LOVE & WAR

MELISSA STORM

EDITOR: STEVIE MIKAYNE

COVER BY ROMANCEPREMADES.COM

PROOFREADER: FALCON STORM

PARTRIDGE & PEAR PRESS

PO BOX 72

BRIGHTON, MI 48116

To Falcon who taught me the meaning of love

WHEN I FALL IN LOVE,
PART I

James raked his toes through the cleanly cut grass. Was this the last time he'd ever enjoy this sensation? Even if he came out of it with his life, he'd be a changed man. Better to enjoy the simple pleasures while he still could.

A powder blue Cadillac pulled into the driveway next door.

Tommy Morrison climbed out of the driver's seat and swooped around to open the passenger side door for his lady friend, Diana. His face lit up when he spied James watching.

"Why, hello, James. Sure is a pretty day, in't it?"

James smiled and nodded, unable to tear his eyes

away as Tommy and Diana kissed right in the driveway for all of the neighborhood to see. He watched as Tommy whispered into her ear, and Diana kicked back her heel in that classic gesture of a woman in love.

It was Tommy's last day of freedom as well. He too would ship off in the morning to answer his country's call. Seemed he'd chosen a very different way to spend the evening.

Love was not something he believed in. Freedom though, now that was the real deal. And malted milk shakes in cool metal glasses—oh, how he'd miss those. Luckily, the local soda fountain was only a short walk into town. He'd have his fill, then return for his last comfortable night at home in his own bed, that's what he'd do.

So he sprang to his feet and headed into town, making sure to pay especially close attention to how the birds chirped from the trees and how the shiny copper of an abandoned penny glistened in the sun, how freedom hung in the air like a fine perfume. He'd miss his country, but he'd also do anything to protect it from the Communist threat.

James pushed open the door to the soda shop, and a tiny bell jingled to greet him. "The usual," he called back into the kitchen. "Plus add an order of French fries, will ya?"

He sat down at the bar to await his meal, his feet jiggling beneath him as they tip-tapped on the checkered linoleum floor.

Then the doorbells jingled again, and the most beautiful woman James had ever seen walked into the shop. The setting sun cast a warm glow on her skin and her eyes glistened even brighter than the copper of that penny. They were a darker shade of the same color, too. Her skirt swished around her calves as she made her way over to the counter and sat down beside James.

Maybe love was every bit as powerful as freedom after all.

Deborah felt the young soldier's eyes fix on her the moment she entered the soda shop. Normally, she'd blush and try to get away, but the sign of his crisply pressed uniform hinted at a boy about to deploy in the fight for her liberties, and she knew better than to deny him the simple pleasure of looking at her, if that's what he wanted to do.

Besides, he wasn't so bad on the eyes himself,

with the high apples of his cheeks and strong, angular jawline. He looked strong all over, from his jaw to his biceps, right down to the stern but welcoming expression he wore on his young, handsome face.

"The name's Morgan, Airman First Class." He stuck his hand out toward her in greeting.

"I'm Deborah. Thank you for serving, Morgan." She smiled sweetly then buried her face in the menu.

"Actually, you should call me James, seeing as it's my first name and all. Care to let me treat you to a malted milk? It would be an honor and a pleasure."

She took a moment to size him up. Deciding he was harmless, she answered with "Strawberry, thank you."

"Hey, that's what I like too. In fact, mine only just came out from back. Take it." He slid the chilly confection her way, and she graciously accepted.

"When do you ship off?" she asked, sucking in a mouthful of the delicious treat as she waited for his answer.

"Tomorrow morning."

"So this is your last night stateside?"

He glanced toward the counter for a moment, then fixed his gaze on her with burning intensity.

"Come out on the town with me, Deborah. Let's make a night to remember."

Deborah smiled and stammered to buy herself some time. She'd only just turned seventeen, and she'd never gone steady with a boy before. But James wasn't asking to go steady. He was just inviting her out for a wholesome night of fun. Who was she to deny him this small pleasure when he was willing to give so much to keep his fellow Americans safe and free?

James tapped his foot on the floor. A nervous twitch? His lips set in a straight line, and she could tell he was forcing himself to keep his mouth shut and let her answer when she felt good and ready.

Well, heck, he seemed like a nice enough fellow. What could one night hurt?

"Okay," she said at last. "Let's hit the town."

James couldn't believe his luck. She'd agreed. This angel had actually agreed to spend the night with plain, old him. He couldn't tear his eyes away from her as they walked down the clean sidewalks of the tiny downtown area, licking at ice cream cones—

strawberry, of course—and getting to know one another.

He banged his arm against a streetlight, but he hardly noticed the throbbing pain as they carried on down the street.

Deborah winced but continued with her story.

"So I graduate next year, and I have no idea what I'll do then. You know, if I were a fella, I think I might like to serve like you're doing. Of course, it'd be the Navy for me though. I do so love the water."

James smiled. "I'm guessin' that's only because you haven't yet seen the skies. Maybe one day I can show you.

"I'd like that."

As they neared the edge of the park, Deborah rushed ahead and climbed onto the brick retaining wall, then placed one foot carefully in front of the other as she balanced on the ledge.

"I haven't seen the skies, but now I'm a little bit closer." She giggled and leaped into James's arms when she reached the end of the wall.

He held her waist and stared into her eyes. His ice cream cone lay melting on the sidewalk beside him, but he didn't mind one bit.

Deborah flushed and scrunched up her nose,

then took a big lick of her still intact cone. "Mmm-mmm," she teased before offering James to share.

And just as quickly as she had ended up in his arms, she was out again. She raced toward the tiny courtyard at the park's center and stopped before the statue of old Huxtable.

"You kind of look like him, don't you?" She moved her eyes from the statue to James then back again.

"Well, that's a first." He laughed. "Never been told I remind someone of an old, dirty statue before."

"You can see it in the jaw." She gently brushed her fingers along his.

He wanted to swoop in and kiss her so badly, but he knew better than to take such liberties with a girl he'd just met—no matter how much he felt for her already.

"Well then, I'm flattered. I hope I can be half the hero Huxtable was."

She reached forward to hold both his hands, and an intoxicating, tingling feeling worked its way through his body.

"To me, you already are."

She liked him. She really liked him. Too much for the welfare of either, she feared. What was it about this man that had her so taken? Was it because she feared for her own future as well as his?

A year until graduation. That's all she had to figure out her place in the world, not that there were too many places where she'd belong.

She hated that the boys were the ones to have all the adventures while her parents expected her to brush up on her domestic skills and find a nice boy to marry. She didn't want to be stuck in a kitchen for the rest of her life. No, she wanted to see the world, on the back of a motorcycle or aboard a sailboat perhaps.

Staying still had never suited her much.

Then there was James. He almost made her want to give up on her delusions of what her life could be and throw them toward the altar of marriage. They'd drink malted milks in bed and take the wildest vacations with their brood of sons.

She could picture their life together already, and it scared her.

What about her freedom? What about her sense of self?

She felt she still had them with James, but would it be the same with another boy? Her parents couldn't afford college, and besides they didn't think she'd need a degree to be a housewife—said her poetry was nothing more than a silly hobby.

But what would James think?

"I write, did you know that?"

He laughed for what was probably the hundredth time since they'd met earlier that evening. "Not until you just told me, but somehow I'm not surprised. Read me something?"

"I'll tell you one of my favorites. I must confess it's a little inappropriate for mixed company."

James's face flushed, but he didn't look away. "I don't mind, if you don't."

She stepped a few paces away, then recited her favorite thing she'd ever written.

> "My love knows no man.
> My love knows only me.
> Touching, feeling, imagining what
>   could one day be.
> My love is hungry, devouring me from
>   inside.
> Yet still I have no partner in whom I
>   can confide.
> To touch, to feel, to live a love so real
>   and full.

One day it may be, but until then
myself I am whole."

James's face was a whole new shade of red as he glanced from her face to her hands, working out the meaning behind her poetry.

"I like that you can be so honest in your writing. You have a real gift, Deborah."

Now she was the one flushing. Her name on his lips was enough to bring the heat to her cheeks as well as other parts of her body as of yet untouched by a man.

His eyes stayed on her as he rose from the bench and closed the distance between them. The stars above twinkled, as did his eyes as he drew nearer.

"May I kiss you?" he asked at last, and she could only nod, her words having been consumed by the poetry.

He inched forward to close the final bit of distance between them. The evening shadow on his chin tickled as they came together, and she liked it very much—the smoothness of his lips matched with the coarseness of his whiskers.

So this is what it feels like to be with a man?

Only she knew it wasn't just about being with a

man. It was about being with James. They'd only just begun, and already she was smitten.

And as soon as the night began, it was over.

Their kiss had been short and sweet and earth-shattering. Why couldn't he have met this perfect woman earlier—or even later? Why did it have to be when so little time remained of his youth—and quite possibly of his life?

He couldn't—nor would he want to—defect. His country needed him, and he was proud to serve. Yet...

Deborah's thumb massaged his as they held hands and strolled through the neighborhood. He'd ask her to go steady, but knowing he'd be gone for so long... that just wouldn't be fair.

It was like caging a wild bird, the beauty being erased by the captivity. He refused to put Deborah in a cage, no matter how much he'd like to keep her as his own.

If things between them were right—as he truly believed them to be—then it would all work out for them in the end, war or no war. They'd find a way back into each other's arms somehow.

"This is me." Deborah pointed toward a small ranch style home with green shutters and a row of rosebushes out front.

This was it, the end of their perfect evening together.

"I don't have a way with words the way you do, but this has been real swell, Deborah. Thank you for coming out with me tonight."

"Swell, indeed."

She smiled, but he could sense the building sorrow behind her mask of happiness. While this could very well be the end for them, he refused to believe it. He hoped she felt the same too.

"May I kiss you goodnight?" he asked.

She shook her head. "Our last kiss was perfect, and I refuse to kiss goodnight, because it's really kissing goodbye."

She took his face in her hands and leaned in to brush her eyelashes against his cheek. "This isn't goodbye, you hear? It's just see ya in a while."

They embraced, and then Deborah headed inside alone.

MY HEART BELONGS TO ONLY YOU

CHAPTER I

Cold. So very cold. Rip's teeth chattered as he hugged his gun to his chest and ran through the hills, doing his best to keep cover in the open terrain. A rain of bullets fell all around him as the enemy drew closer. He tore off his glove with his teeth and tried to radio for help, but the frigid air had sucked the life from its battery. Not even static answered his calls for more men.

"We're all we've got," George said from beside him. "So we've gotta be enough."

Rip nodded. He wanted to communicate something more, but each staggered breath brought searing pain. The icy air entered his nostrils like sharp claws trying to grab onto his heart and tear it out. It would save the commies the trouble.

With all the resolve he could muster, he crept toward the enemy encampment on the horizon. His breath poured out of him, a disjointed stream of dragon smoke when what he really needed was fire —anything to warm him up.

More bullets.

George let out a sharp cry and pulled away from him at a rapid clip.

Rip tried to keep up, but the ice had gotten to his muscles—and now held on tight, forcing him to take short, quick steps rather than the long bounds he needed to provide backup for his buddy.

More bullets. A warmth blossoming out from the center of his chest, a warmth which failed to bring relief. Sharp pain, and he fell to his side, clutching at his heart and praying for a quick death.

George continued forward, jack-rabbiting across the field. He raised his gun to take aim, and then... nothing. The bullets would not come. "Ice jammed it up!" he shouted and tried to fall back.

More bullets. Coming at George rather than from his gun.

Rip watched in fear as his closest friend buckled at the knees and fell face-forward into the earth, the last thing he saw before everything went white.

He kicked furiously and shot up with a start. The winter landscape fell away revealing an empty room with dull brown walls and no windows. He sucked air in and pushed it out easily. Cold droplets of sweat clung to his skin, and only the phantom memory of wounds past pained him. Seconds before, they had been so real.

The nightmare was always the same, coming to him with such vivid detail he had no choice but to relive that battle every night since he'd so narrowly escaped with his life. Sometimes he needn't even fall asleep. Just shutting his eyes drew out the carnage, reminded him how his failure to keep up had cost George his life.

He couldn't run then, but he could certainly run now. And he would. If he ran far enough, perhaps he could finally escape the memory.

A soft knock sounded at the door. Tuesdays were her mother's salon days, and she attended them as fervently as she did church on Sundays, which meant the task of answering the caller would fall to Deborah. She forced herself up from bed, tugged a housecoat over her shoulders, and padded to the door.

A man in uniform stood before her, his arm fastened into a sling. "Ma'am," he said by way of greeting.

"Yes? How can I help you?" She tried—and failed —to stifle a yawn. Exactly how early was it anyway?

"I'm Airman First Class Morrison—or Tommy. Are you Deborah Walker?"

"I am. What's this about?"

"I.... Well, I'm a friend of James Morgan."

Fear flooded Deborah's heart. She couldn't remember moving, but somehow she and Tommy ended up in the living room sharing tea as if they were sitting together for a nice, friendly visit, and not...

Finally she spoke. "Is James...?" She refused to finish the question. Words held power, after all, and she wouldn't lend them any extra in this situation.

"Dead?" Tommy steepled his fingers before his chest, taking a painful pause.

Deborah wanted to shake him hard until the answer to her question spilled out, but she didn't have the strength enough to say anything.

"No, but he is missing in action, ma'am. Some people say that's as good as, but I know ol' Jimmy, and he had too much fight in him to surrender."

Deborah remained quiet as the information sank in. For months she had waited for him and with only a single letter to tide her over. Had he been missing all this time? Was he...? No, she refused to even think it.

"Anyway, I thought you should know before the public caught wind. Seeing as you were his girl and all."

"Thank you very much, Airman," she muttered, keeping her eyes fixed on his freshly polished shoes.

He said a few other things, but she didn't catch them. And after a while she watched as Tommy's shoes carried themselves up and out of her house.

One night, one kiss, one memory where he was hers. That was all Deborah got before life—or quite possibly death—took her love away from her. If she were more the religious type, she'd believe God had decided to have some fun at her expense. Instead, she chose to think this was just the way the world worked in these terrible days, which were filled to the brim with war.

Still, she prayed James would find his way back to her safe and sound, that they would one day be together for good. Just in case there was a God, and he was concerned enough to help her out.

Chapter 2

"What we have here is a classic case of shell shock," the doctor had explained before handing Rip a brochure to outline the finer points of his diagnosis.

He found the brochure now wedged in between Orwell and Camus on his sparsely populated bookshelf. He'd once taken pride in his possessions, kept them meticulously arranged—but this place no longer felt like home, and his possessions now all seemed like someone else's things.

Remember, the doctor had said, *sometimes the best medicine is time.*

But how much time? And would the wounds ever fully heal or would his mind be forever scarred, his heart forever empty? Rip ran his fingers over his chest, scratching at the fleshy scars on his chest. Sometimes digging his nails in caused enough physical pain to give him a temporary reprieve from the tremendous sense of guilt he carried everywhere he went.

The relief never lasted though. The moment his

pain ebbed away, the hollowness returned. Time had done nothing to heal those particular wounds, but perhaps distance would.

He hauled another box onto the bedframe and tossed in clothes, books, linens—whatever lay nearby.

"Do it for George," he muttered to himself. He had to get better and quick so he could return to the front lines and fight in his fallen friend's honor. And that's why he was moving away from base now. Seeing the active servicemen go about their duties only added to his sense of longing. At least they were being productive, contributing to the greater good, while Rip simply waited for his head to straighten out so the doc would clear him to return to war. Rip had become a shell of what he was supposed to be, which was fitting—he supposed—since it fit the diagnosis and all.

He dug into the back of his closet and fished out a photo of George and him with the rest of their troop mates. After carrying the crinkled portrait over to the half-filled box, he tossed it instead into the waste bin at the other end of the room.

Memories of adventures past weren't what he needed. He needed an escape.

A normal life, a boring one. *That's* what he

needed to get better. But how could he return to normalcy when the very substance of who he'd been oozed out from him as he lay dying on that icy field in Korea? One way or another he'd figure things out. His sense of honor depended on it.

A year had passed since she'd learned of James's disappearance—four seasons, twelve months, fifty-two weeks, and infinite heartbreaks. Deborah had become a modern-day Prometheus. Each day the vultures of loss tore her heart to pieces, and each night the Gods cruelly restored it, forcing her to suffer the same fate anew.

She held tight to that solid brass ring of hope. Maybe it would be enough to pull her from the depths of sorrow. Maybe her faith would be rewarded, and James would return home unscathed and still full of love for her.

It seemed she was alone in her optimism, though. The town had already held a memorial service for James and the other hometown boys who'd failed to return home. She'd been too afraid to introduce herself to his mother who sat in the front pew, dabbing at her tears with a lace-embroidered hanky. What good would revealing herself to the grieving mother do, telling the unknown woman how she'd once hoped—still hoped, in fact—to marry her son?

A year was a very long time to wait without receiving any news. Sometimes she wished they could at least find James's body and give her some closure—but she realized how terribly selfish such a wish was and she hated herself for so much as thinking it.

And just as the status of James's life was on hold, so too was the future of hers. Her parents didn't have enough money to send her to college, and, besides which, they didn't really see the purpose of educating a woman when her main role would always be inside the home—much to Deborah's chagrin. She'd fought hard for her right to be taken seriously, to be sent to college where she could work toward pursuing her passion for writing professionally, but at the same time, the money just wasn't there.

Everything had changed when she'd met James, though. He almost made her parents' old-fashioned ways seem right. She'd found herself daydreaming about life as James's wife, sharing strawberry milkshakes in bed, exchanging jokes and secrets well into their golden years.

It would've been a good life. *It still could be*, she chided herself. Hope. She could still hope.

Deborah frowned as she continued through the neighborhood on the seat of her bicycle, riding in that awkward time of day when the sun got into her eyes no matter where she directed her gaze.

Most days she volunteered her time at the nursing home. It only seemed fitting since she had so much to spare, and the residents had so little of their own remaining. Besides, she spent most of her visiting hours reading them books, and, occasionally, she'd even slip in something of her own—a new dime novel she'd procured from the corner pharmacy or a poem she'd written in her head on the ride over. The residents never seemed to mind.

Reading and writing were both lonely habits, but they seemed much less so whenever she could find a way to share them with others.

She constructed the next verse of a poem as she rode, but found herself hopelessly stuck on a particularly tricky couplet. Although she generally wrote in free form, if she chose to follow a rhyme scheme, she refused to sully it with lazy almost-rhymes.

Now what would work perfectly with *forward she*

marches with a heart long besieged? The possibilities churned in her mind, but before Deborah could land on the perfect complement, the slam of a screen door caught her attention.

She slowed her bike to a roll and searched for the source of the noise. Almost instantly her eyes landed upon a boxy truck parked in front of the Suttons' old place. The rear hung open, exposing a hodgepodge of stark brown boxes, none of which appeared to be labeled.

"Who on earth...?" she wondered aloud, letting the thought hang before her, unfinished. Well, regardless, a new neighbor had come to town, which meant she'd need to pass along her family's welcome, and soon. She'd give the new resident tonight to finish unpacking, then return bright and early with a freshly baked batch of her mother's famous blueberry muffins. After all, it was the neighborly thing to do—and, for Deborah, maintaining these small niceties went a long way toward keeping herself stable as the earth spun dangerously fast beneath her feet.

CHAPTER 3

The doorbell rang.

Rip dragged a hand across his forehead and stood. He'd been hard at work hauling boxes and furniture all morning and had very nearly finished moving into his new temporary home, a small Craftsman with two bedrooms and no bathtub.

Neighbors had been dropping by all morning with steaming hot casseroles and fresh fruit baskets, eagerly peering over his shoulder when he opened the door to accept their greetings—clearly interested in learning more about him, but only for the sake of gossip. He'd thought old Mrs. Thompson had been the last of them and he could finally focus on his work, when the bell rang again.

"Someone's impatient," he muttered to himself as he shuffled toward the door. His T-shirt clung to his chest, glued down with stale sweat. If the sight of him didn't scare away this new gawker, perhaps the stench would.

He grabbed the knob and yanked the door open, startling the petite blonde who stood on his porch holding a large wicker basket. The smile fell from her face almost instantly, but still she was much more pleasant to look at than old Mrs. Thompson or any of the others who had been by that morning.

"Can I help you with something?" he prompted when she failed to introduce herself.

A flush rose over her cheeks and she pushed the basket into his arms. "Hi, I'm Deborah Walker, and I'd like to personally welcome you to the neighborhood." She smiled, apparently relieved to have delivered her lines in this skit of social niceties.

Rip lifted the corner of the checkered cloth that covered the contents of the basket. The delicious scent of brown sugar and blueberries escaped into the air, mixing with the stench of sweat and sawdust surrounding him. "With muffins," he stated.

"Yes, with muffins." Deborah smiled, though it seemed forced now.

Apparently he was doing a poor job keeping up his end of the exchange.

"Like I said, I'm Deborah Walker. And who might you be?"

He took a deep breath before replying. He was far too tired to have to deal with this right now. Even if he wanted to, he wouldn't be able to sweep the pretty, young woman away with his charm. He didn't have it in him. "Sergeant First Class Rip Rockwell. How ya doing?"

"Oh, um." She tucked a stray curl behind her ear

and looked awkwardly at her feet. "Well, I'm sure I'll see you around town. Enjoy the muffins."

He raised his hand to wave goodbye, but she had already taken off down the walkway and back toward the street.

Oh, well. He needed to get back to work anyway. The last thing Rip needed was excitement, least of all that which only a woman could provide. He took a moment to re-imagine the scene that had played out on his porch, to pretend he had invited her in and served sweet tea, that they had engaged in witty repartee, had made a date for the weekend.

No matter. Their love story wasn't meant to be, and that was fine by him. Less trouble meant a quicker recovery; it meant returning to his country's call, avenging his fallen friend. It meant staying away from Deborah Walker at all costs.

Deborah kicked the quilt off her bed as she turned over once again. For some reason her brain simply refused to shut off for the night, and she was pretty sure this reason was the handsome—albeit *rude*—new neighbor.

"With muffins," he had said, teasing her for her

hospitality. Only he *wasn't* teasing. Teasing would imply he cared enough to have a go at her. No, his face and tone had both remained flat the entire time she'd stood before him on his porch, doing her best to make a good impression for the sake of her family's reputation in the neighborhood.

A lot of good that did.

So why couldn't she just brush off his indifference and move on? He hadn't been openly hostile toward her. He hadn't been interested in making any friends, at least not making friends with her.

Sergeant First Class Rip Rockwell back on home soil while there was a war on. There had to be a reason for that. Had he been dishonorably discharged and stripped of his title but still bullishly clung to it anyway?

He didn't seem the dishonorable sort. He didn't seem the friendly sort either, but still.

Why did she care so much? *Aargh*.

"Because he's handsome," a small voice whispered in her head. "Because he reminds you of James." She hated to admit it, but she also couldn't hide the truth from her own consciousness. The inner Deborah knew what the outer Deborah was loath to admit.

She closed her eyes and pictured him before her

—the sharp jawline, the high and tight haircut, the two-day stubble lining his cheeks. Would it scratch her if they were to kiss, or would it tickle instead?

Stop thinking like that. Think of something else, anything else. Or, better yet, get some sleep. Lord knows you need it.

She flipped over in bed again and thought of his strong arms as they accepted the muffin basket...of his plump lower lip and those gorgeous hazel eyes.

Yes, it was definitely the eyes. They were just like James's. No wonder she couldn't get Rip out of her head. Not because she liked *him*. Only that she missed James. So why couldn't she picture any part of her lost lover besides his familiar eyes?

She was forgetting him already—and, for that, she was deeply ashamed.

Okay, there's no way I'm getting back to sleep, she finally admitted to herself as she set both of her bare feet onto the plush carpeting below. Perhaps a few quick laps to clear her head?

She shrugged off her pajamas and stepped into her swimming costume, then pulled a dress over top. Nothing quite cleared her head the way swimming did. It was why she'd always loved the water almost as much as she loved the written word.

Yes, a quick swim would set her straight. Perhaps

afterward she'd compose some new verses. She had far too much to do to lose sleep over some rude former soldier.

Time to move on.

CHAPTER 4

It wouldn't stop snowing. White fluff rained down from above while bullets flew in from every other direction. Rip was stuck, hopelessly stuck. George ran ahead, and—

"NOOOO!" Rip screamed and jerked forward after his too-brave-for-his-own-good friend. But George disappeared in an instant, replaced by a looming wall of beige. Rip's legs regained their mobility and kicked the blanket of snow from his body.

So cold, yet so hot at the same time.

It's just my bedroom, he realized, surveying his surroundings with caution. Then why did it still feel so much like he was back in Korea? Why'd he feel as if he'd never left the country, never left that single moment in time when he...and George...?"

He had to escape. Somehow he had to find a way to shake off the guilt that clung to him like a bad cologne, following him everywhere, reminding him of his failure to act, of the mistakes that had cost another's life.

Why couldn't he get away? Why couldn't he scrub his conscience clean once and for all?

Well, thinking wasn't getting him anywhere. He needed to act instead. Rip attempted to clear his mind—or at least to dull George's screams to a whisper—as he pulled on a shirt and padded outside into the pre-dawn air.

He walked slowly, hesitantly at first, then all of a sudden he was running—as if moving fast enough could turn back time, make everything different, better. In time, he found himself at the lake. He'd heard there was one nearby but hadn't cared enough to find it before now. Luckily, its glistening coolness was exactly what he needed to wash away the guilt, the fear, the anger.

He stripped off his shirt and shorts, wanting to feel the redeeming current glide over every inch of his body, allowing nothing to stand between him and a bit of relief. The clothes came off, and he ran again, straight into the arms of the waiting lake, its water dark and calm under the light of the few remaining stars. The water took him, held him, and for a while he did feel better. But soon his lungs began to burn, forcing him to return to the surface and face the larger world once more.

As soon as he did, something felt...wrong.

He spun around, searching the horizon for the source of danger he sensed so acutely. Small ripples pushed through the water and approached his exposed body. He followed them back until he found the source. There, just a few feet farther into the lake, a woman stared at him, eyes large with shock, mouth parted ever so slightly, wet hair plastered to her shoulders.

The muffin woman had definitely just gotten to know him on a far more intimate basis.

First shock, then humiliation, and final arousal buoyed inside Deborah as she treaded water and stared at Sergeant Rip Rockwell, here and very much in the flesh.

So that's what a naked man looks like, she thought. Not bad. Not bad at all. Don't stare now. He's probably embarrassed too. Say something... Anything!

But words wouldn't come, and even though his intimate bits had been on display but a moment as Rip darted from the shore into the cool water, they had definitely made a lasting impression on Deborah. Everything about him seemed immaculately put together, as if his body were a fine work of art that had taken its maker years to sculpt. Tiny ripples moved through the water, crashing into his biceps and disappearing. Droplets of water clung to the ends of his eyelashes, giving him a vulnerable appearance she rather liked. His face, though, remained a mask devoid of any real emotion.

Deborah weighed the options in her mind. She could make a break for it, pretend this awkward encounter never happened. But still, her swimming costume didn't leave an awful lot to the imagination, and traipsing back up the shore while he watched would only compound the embarrassment for both of them—of that much, she was sure. *She*'d done nothing out of sorts here. She could respond with grace under pressure, put him at ease, as if it were no big deal she'd seen his privates, first class though they were.

Well, this is ridiculous. One of us has to say something. But what? Deborah chose to go with the first thing that popped into her mind.

"A war injury?" she asked, clutching a hand to

her chest, marking the place where his skin had been silvery and rough.

He shook his head and looked toward shore, then answered so quietly she almost didn't make out his words. "I don't like to talk about it."

Heat bloomed in her chest. Of course, he didn't want to talk about it. Now she was the one being rude. It wasn't her place to pry, nor was it her place to demand anything of a man who had so selflessly served their country in their time of need.

"Did you like the muffins?" She smiled to show she truly meant no harm.

He laughed, and somehow the whole sky lit up in response. "I ate four of them for supper last night. Best darn muffins I ever tasted."

The response didn't surprise her, but still she was happy to hear the enthusiasm in his voice. "Oh, good. Mother will be so pleased."

"Yes, please give her my thanks and accept my apologies." His voice dropped to a whisper once more. "I didn't think anyone else would be out here this early. I obviously didn't mean to—"

"Don't worry about it. Could happen to anyone. Well, maybe not *anyone*, but still."

Now they were both laughing. The vibrations of which created even larger ripples. She hadn't felt so light, so carefree, since her night with James. Of course, thinking of James brought guilt, which immediately soured her mood.

"Well, it was nice, uhh, seeing you, Sergeant Rockwell. I really best be off. Would you mind...?" She twirled her finger in the air to motion for him to turn around.

"Oh, oh, yes, of course." He swam off toward the opposite shore, and Deborah raced to her towel. "Have a nice day!" she called back to Rip as she started on the path toward home.

CHAPTER 5

After his swim, Rip returned to his new house and took up with George Orwell, but he found it difficult to focus on *Animal Farm* and all its not-so-subtle symbolism, because his mind kept running back to the girl, back to Deborah.

He placed the book down on the arm of his chair and tried to conjure her image in his mind. The large, blond curls, the smooth, pale skin with a sun-kissed blush, the slope of her long neck, her slender frame which appeared far more buxom in her swimming costume than it had the afternoon before. Yes,

Deborah Walker was a looker all right, and oh how he wanted to be able to look again.

Their meeting that morning, though, had been brief, and they hadn't made plans to meet again. He'd already thanked her for the muffins, so arriving at her doorstep to thank her again was out of the question. Besides which, he didn't even know where her doorstep might be.

He read about Snowball and Napoleon some more, but the words weren't sticking. *Shoot.*

Well, he couldn't sit here all day and do nothing. Thoughts of Deborah were driving him crazy, and he was already crazy enough on his own. He had to find her, if only to satisfy his blistering desire to see her again.

Perhaps that would be enough.

But as he laced up his Oxfords and put on a light jacket, he knew this wouldn't be the case. Something about Deborah had reached a part of him—which part? Well, that had yet to be determined. Only time —and perhaps another impromptu run-in—would tell.

Rip strolled through the neighborhood and headed downtown. He didn't know this town well enough yet to know where to look, so he decided to go wherever his feet took him. After all, they had delivered him to the right place earlier that morning, right?

The soda shop drew him in with its checked floors and shiny metal accents. Fresh grilled burgers and fried potatoes filled his nostrils and made his stomach growl. He made a note to return later. Perhaps with Deborah, if she'd have him.

But she wasn't there now, so he continued through town in search of her.

He smiled at another wounded vet and held the door open for him so he didn't have to struggle with his crutches. Must be nice, Rip thought, having your injuries visible for all to see. But then he immediately felt guilty. This man was hurt same as him, and it wasn't his place to judge—the same way he didn't want others feeling sorry for him when they found out about his head or his heart.

That's when he realized he hadn't thought of George the entire morning, not since running into Deborah at the lake. Instead, his constant, terrifying flashbacks had been replaced with Deborah's laugh, Deborah's smile.

He'd assumed a woman was the last thing he needed. Could it be that a woman—and not just any woman, but Deborah—was the *only* thing he needed to finally become himself again?

I will find her. I will, he told himself as he continued to weave through the tiny downtown area. Soon the buildings began to fade, giving way to greenery—trees, rose gardens, and daffodils. He walked past a large retaining wall that helped to separate the park on his right from the traffic on his left.

Just as he was about to turn around and begin his search anew, he spotted her. She sat on a bench seat staring up at a statue of the town's founder while nibbling the end of her ink pen. A journal sat open on her lap, which was covered with a sunny, yellow dress—a dress Rip liked very much. He liked everything about her, actually. He hung back to watch her and to think of how he might get her to return his affections.

How hard could it be to attract a woman's interest?

Deborah's shift ended early that day. The seniors were having a special in-home sock hop that afternoon, and, even though they'd begged her to stay, she hated to intrude on their fun. She also didn't want to steal a spot in the partner line-up when the women already outnumbered the men at least three to one.

So, instead of staying or heading straight home, Deborah decided to visit Huxtable in the park downtown. Ever since James had left for war, she'd come here often to think of him and the kiss they'd shared in this very spot. When he went missing, she began coming here even more often to retain a connection with him...and to mourn.

She'd tried so many times to write a poem about their love story, but she always came up short. Was that because their story hadn't finished yet? Or because her heart was too broken to make sense of what they'd had?

"Well, old Huxtable, it seems you are the best friend I have left," she told the statue in her mind. "Thanks for always being here."

The stone face of the town's founder stared over her head, an unmovable expression on his face. Although she never expected him to answer, it still made her sad when the stone man failed to come to life and reciprocate her friendship.

"Why can't I ever find the right words to describe James?" she continued to carry on the one-sided conversation in her head. "I can write about every-thing else, so why not the one thing that matters most? Between you and me, I feel like a sham of a writer. But I also can't stop trying, no matter how bad the block gets. Silly me." She sighed and stared down at her empty notebook again.

"Deborah!" a man called from across the way.

She blinked up at Huxtable, confused until she saw Rip striding toward her.

"H-hello," she answered, rising to face him and tittering nervously. "We can't keep meeting like this." Somehow the blank pages of her journal embarrassed her, as if Rip could sense the words she'd wanted to confide in its pages yet had failed to find.

"Hi. Mind if I join you?" he asked, motioning toward the bench.

She sat back down and crossed her legs at the ankles, then patted the seat beside her. "Sure. Have a seat."

"Were you writing something?" he asked. "I mean, I don't want to pry, but you just looked so thoughtful. I didn't want to interrupt, but I also did want to interrupt, know what I mean?" He smiled, showing off two rows of glistening white teeth.

Deborah thought she caught a wink, but had a hard time reconciling the forward, flirty man before her with the one she'd met on either of their two previous run-ins. "I...Well, I was trying to, but—"

"Writer's block?" He seemed almost too eager.

"Unfortunately, yes." She groaned. "My creativity's been a bit lacking since..."

This time the silence lingered between them.

"Since the war?"

Deborah nodded.

"Did you lose somebody you loved?" he asked. Genuine sympathy shone in his eyes despite the fact she could bet he'd lost far more than she.

"That's the thing." Her voice caught. "I don't know. James was declared MIA about a year ago, and I haven't heard anything since. Sometimes I wish I could at least know one way or the other, rather than waiting in this constant purgatory, but then I feel guilty, as if it would be my fault, if..."

"You don't have to finish. I understand." Rip smiled at Deborah and swung his feet back and forth in an attempt to lighten the mood.

"Look at me." She forced a laugh and swiped at her eyes. "Crying in public like this."

"It's okay. I understand. The war's been hard on us all."

"Oh, gosh, I didn't even—I mean, you must have—"

"Really, it's okay. And you're right. It's been hard on me too. I lost my best friend, couldn't do anything to stop it, though I tried. And whenever I close my eyes, I see him taking his final breath. I see him falling to the ground and not getting back up again." The smile vanished from Rip's face and his eyes, which had been focused on her, stared blankly across the park.

"Now they say I have shell shock, that I'm unfit to serve when serving is the only way I can make things right again."

Deborah nodded. As much as the war had hurt her, she knew she could never fully understand what Rip was going through. All she could do was be there for him as he tried to work things out.

The ease with which she realized her need to support this new man in her life startled her. She was still in mourning for James, yet she so easily found herself interested in the literal next man who came along and showed her even the smallest bit of kindness. "What was his name? Your friend?"

"George," Rip answered, having difficulty speaking the name aloud.

"Tell me about him."

If he was surprised by her request, he didn't let on. Instead Rip's face came back to life as he recounted tales of his and George's childhoods. "We did everything together," he said. "Even enlisted together. The only thing we didn't do is come back home together. Makes me wonder why I'm still here, why I would survive when he didn't."

"Like there's some greater purpose?" Deborah prompted.

He shrugged. "I don't know about that. But it's nice to think maybe... I don't know. Surviving feels like a huge burden, as if it's up to me to make the most of my life as well as what his could have been."

"Like you can never be free again?" she asked. "I know what that feels like too."

Rip looked up at her. The tenderness left his expression, and his features scrunched together. "Jeez, I'm sorry. You were probably having a perfectly nice afternoon, before I came over here and unloaded my problems on you. I'll let you get back to your writing."

Watching Rip fret forced Deborah to realize she could either resume living her life or she could keep things forever on hold while she awaited news of James, a man she had loved but who was no longer here.

While she took solace in Huxtable's company, she didn't want to be like the old statue. She was still young, alive, full of life, and completely capable of living it.

Rip stood to go, but she placed a hand on his wrist. "Stay."

"You wouldn't mind?"

"Not at all. Despite what you think, you're good company. Sit back down, or actually...have you ever been to the cliff?"

"The cliff? Which cliff?"

Deborah giggled. "*The* cliff, and I'll take it you *haven't* been. C'mon, we're going to change that right now." She grabbed his hand and pulled him up again, hesitating when it was time to let go. She so liked feeling the warmth of his fingers between hers, the sound of his voice in her ear, the simple pleasure of his company.

Maybe she could fall in love again after all.

CHAPTER 6

Rip followed Deborah up the incline, admiring the way her skirt swished about her calves. They exited the forest path and found themselves in the middle of a huge open field adorned with rocks of all shapes and sizes. The slope of the hill they'd climbed cut away, revealing a shining lake beneath.

"Well, here we are," Deborah announced,

glancing back at him from over her shoulder, the joy in her expression barely contained. "Don't you adore it? When you were telling me about George and about feeling trapped, I knew I had to bring you. I feel freer here than pretty much anywhere else in the world."

She ran through the grass with her arms at her sides like wings. "C'mon." She reached her hands toward him and motioned for him to join.

He grabbed hold of her soft fingers for the second time that afternoon. He hadn't realized he'd been so tired, not until her touch jolted him awake. Something about Deborah energized him in a way nothing had been able to since the war had broken out.

She pulled him forward and swung herself in a kind of dance, laughing as the breeze tousled her curls, then spun away and headed toward the edge of the cliff. "The best part is the moment between when you jump and when you hit the water, because it's just like flying."

"Did you bring your swimming costume?" Rip glanced at the small purse she'd brought with her.

"Nope. Don't need one, but do me a favor and turn around."

She wasn't going to…?

"No peeking!" she cried.

She was, she was actually disrobing right in front of—well, actually right *behind*—him.

"Okay, now turn around. But keep your eyes closed!"

She came close and he could feel her breath on his face. He considered leaning in for a kiss, but something told him the time wasn't right just yet. Instead, he did as he was told and kept his eyes firmly shut.

"Good. Now take off your shirt and pants," she instructed.

He chuckled. "Will you close your eyes?"

"Of course not. Somebody's gotta make sure you keep yours closed. Besides, I've already seen ...well, you know what happened this morning. Now off with your pants, let's have them."

Rip again did as he was told, and Deborah's laughter stopped abruptly as he slipped his linen shirt off and over his head. He wondered if she was looking at his scars, but he didn't want to ruin the lightheartedness of this moment by taking them back to that dark place. "Okay, now what?"

Deborah tugged him by the arm. "Trust me, okay?"

He swallowed hard. "Okay."

"On the count of three, we're going to jump. It's about a fifteen foot drop, but the water is plenty deep. You'll love it, I promise."

Rip had never much cared for heights, but the war had toughened him. Besides he liked Deborah too much to say no, especially now that they were each dressed only in their undergarments.

She let go of his right hand, but continued to cling to his left. "Take three steps forward." She paused and waited for him. "Okay, one more."

He took another small step toward the cliff's edge.

"Okay, one and a half... Perfect. Are you ready?"

"Yep." His heart banged in his chest, whether from the thrill of the jump before him or the simple joy of being near to Deborah, he couldn't say for sure. Whatever the reason, he liked it. He liked it a lot.

"One." Deborah squeezed his hand as if maybe she were a little bit afraid too.

"Two." Rip took a deep breath and readied his muscles for the jump.

"Three."

And suddenly they were flying through the air, her hold on his hand the only thing anchoring him to the world. He felt incredible. He felt free, exactly as she said he would.

Right before they splashed into the water, she let go of his hand and he opened his eyes a crack to take a peek. He only caught sight of the nearby peach blur of Deborah for an instant before they both splashed into the water below.

Rip let himself sink as far as the dive would propel him, then he hugged his legs to his chest and allowed the water to swish and bubble around him as he sat secure within its hold. He opened his eyes and looked up at the sun, a bright spot lighting the cool darkness. Normally he would hold his breath until his lungs ached for air, if only to remind himself he were still alive, still capable of drawing in another breath, of facing another day. But today he didn't need that reminder. Today being with Deborah was enough.

He let go of his legs and let out a strong practiced kick to take him back to the surface.

"Didn't you just love it?" Her call sounded far away, but when he opened his eyes she treaded only a couple feet from him.

He wracked his brain for the perfect way to tell her what the jump had meant to him, what she was quickly coming to mean too, but before he could find the right words, Deborah closed the small distance between them and shyly kissed him on the cheek.

The kiss lasted only a moment, but its imprint lingered on his skin. He brought his hand up to touch the place where Deborah's lips had been.

"I hope you don't think me too forward," she started. "But I had to—"

Rip didn't mean to interrupt, but he couldn't wait another second to taste Deborah's sweet mouth with his own.

❧

Maple sugar, Deborah decided. That's what Rip's lips tasted like. And as far as kisses went, theirs was extraordinary. Of course, she'd only ever been kissed once before, and that one had been extraordinary too.

She pulled away and offered a shy giggle. As much as she wanted to remain locked in Rip's embrace all day, all night, all eternity, it would hardly be proper—especially considering how few garments they each wore at the time. Letting this continue would simply be begging for impropriety, and Deborah wasn't sure how she'd react if Rip were to make a formal proposition of her.

"C'mon, I'll race you back to shore." She sent a big splash in his direction and continued to laugh as she crawled toward land as fast as her arms would take her.

Rip pulled ahead and scrambled onto shore. "Need me to close my eyes again?"

"I think you'd better."

She emerged from the lake, shivering as the cool wind tickled her thighs. Her white cotton undergarments clung to her skin, hiding neither the taut peaks of her nipples or the dark hairs between her legs. Rip faced away from her to give her the privacy she needed, and she made sure to admire his exposed form as she darted past him and back up to the top of the cliff where they had left their clothing. Though his legs were on the skinny side, his muscular arms and chest more than made up for this slight shortcoming. Despite her curiosity, she averted her eyes from the silver scarring on his torso. After all, if he'd made the effort to respect her privacy, she should do the same.

"Can I come up yet?" he called as she fastened the last of the buttons on her dress.

"One sec!" On second thought, Deborah unfastened her bra and slipped it through the arm hole on her dress then shimmied neatly out of her completely soaked panties. "Okay!"

Rip reached the top of the cliff and grabbed up his clothes while she arranged her undergarments on a large flat rock that lay directly in the path of the sun's light. He looped his arms through his shirt, but left his pants off. "Just until I dry off a bit," he said. "Do you need to get back home, or...?" He let his question linger.

"I've got no place in particular I need to be. I can keep you company while you dry." She carefully situated herself on a smooth patch of grass, taking care to cover her legs with her skirt.

Rip plopped down beside her and arranged his shirt over his lap. "Thanks for bringing me here. You were right, I do love it."

"I knew you would." She smiled, and for a moment felt saddened she'd never gotten the chance to bring James to the cliff. "Mother says I may as well have been born with gills stuck to the sides of my head, seeing how at home I am in the water."

"I've noticed. You've got one heck of a breast stroke."

"Crawl, actually." She blushed. "One day I hope to live right on the ocean, so I can be near the water all the time. And I want to have my very own dinghy. Maybe take a year off, and sail around the world a few times."

"That sounds... wonderful. But, hey, are you sure you wouldn't get bored stuck on a tiny boat for months on end?"

She plucked a violet from the field and twirled it between her fingertips as they talked. "Nope. Not one bit. I'll have my writing and hopefully some good company too."

"Sounds like you have it all figured out." He leaned back on his arms and sighed.

"What? Don't you?"

He shrugged. "'Fraid not. Not anymore."

"Since...?"

"The war, yeah. And not knowing if it's going to be over before I can get back."

"You're more than just a soldier, Sergeant Rockwell. I mean no offense, but nobody is defined by one single thing. We're each a giant cluster of likes and dislikes, hopes and dreams. You're no different than anybody else in that way."

"Maybe, but you should probably call me Rip. Sergeant is a tad more formal than I'd like us to be with each other." He smiled.

"Okay, *Rip.*" She smiled too. "Tell me, what's in your cluster?"

"I don't know. I guess...music. I used to dream of being in a band. Only I can't play an instrument, and I definitely can't dance around on a stage."

"Can you sing?"

"A little."

"Oh, please. Oh, please. Won't you sing for me?" She clasped her hands together and batted her eyelashes.

He laughed and swept a hand through his hair. "Okay. Tell me what you like."

"I've always loved the crooners. Nat King Cole, especially."

"Any particular song?"

She shook her head. "Surprise me."

Rip didn't hesitate for a moment. He sang softly at first, gaining volume as he progressed through the lyrics. Saying he could sing but a little was likely the largest understatement Deborah had ever heard. The words escaped his lips and swirled about them in a beautiful *acapella* symphony as he serenaded her with *Mona Lisa*.

When he reached the part where Nat wonders if his lady love smiles to hide her broken heart, Rip reached a hand to her cheek and let it linger. And as he sang the words asking if she were really truly real, he let the music fade away and focused every bit of his energy onto Deborah, onto gazing into her eyes.

And she gazed right on back. If she hadn't fallen for him already, his song would surely have captured her interest and held on tight. The softness of his voice, the emotion he put behind the words, she'd never heard anything more beautiful in her entire life.

Because she didn't know what to say, she leaned in and kissed him instead.

"So you liked it?" he asked, tucking a fallen curl behind her ear.

"Very, very much so. You're incredibly talented."

"Aww, shucks." A slight blush rose to his cheeks and he looked away, failing to hide his embarrassment. "Now it's your turn. Tell me about *your* cluster."

"Well, I guess it's only fair, isn't it?" She pushed herself up to her feet and crossed the field to retrieve her journal.

"Well, you did start it," Rip teased.

She sat back down beside him and allowed him to pull her tight into his chest. "This is a poem I wrote about a year ago." she explained. She wanted to share something happy, something beautiful—

just as he had done with his song—but her words had been stilted and bleak ever since James's disappearance.

So she chose to read him the same poem she had shared with James. It seemed like an entire lifetime ago. After all, it was still her favorite thing she'd ever written. And though she knew the words by heart, she kept her eyes glued to the page until she'd recited every single word.

> "My love knows no man.
> My love knows only me.
> Touching, feeling, imagining what
>   could one day be.
> My love is hungry, devouring me from
>   inside.
> Yet still I have no partner in whom I
>   can confide.
> To touch, to feel, to live a love so real
>   and full.
> One day it may be, but until then,
>   myself, I am whole."

When she peeked up again, Rip was staring at her, mouth agape. "Is that poem about...?"

Heat rose to her cheeks and to the moist triangle between her legs. "Yes," she answered pertly.

"So you don't—you haven't."

"Of course not, silly!" She pushed at him playfully, feeling the need to gain a bit of proper distance again. "But you didn't tell me. Did you like it?"

"Best darn piece of literature I've ever seen or heard. Now please, please, come back here and give me another kiss."

Deborah laughed but complied all the same, and she and Rip stayed together on that grassy cliff—laughing, kissing, and sharing their passions with one another—until the Texas stars splashed onto the sky's darkening canvas above. Then, Rip walked her back to her doorstep, and they said good-night.

And, oh, what a *good* night it had been.

CHAPTER 7

Rip fell into a deep sleep after returning Deborah to her doorstep, happily exhausted from the afternoon they'd shared in one another's company. He startled awake when the first rays of the morning's sun exploded through his window in perfect sync with the part of his recurring dream where he watched George's body fall to the frozen earth.

He pushed his way through the terror to find the far happier memory of Deborah's kiss. As much as he hated to admit it, George lived in his past whereas Deborah resided in the here and now. He refused to think about the future; after all, it was far too soon to tell which of them he'd be spending it with.

For a moment, he felt sad as he pictured his body in a simple pine casket with an American flag draped on top, Deborah wiping away tears with a hanky as yet another suitor was lost to the war. What would become of her then? Would she turn into an old biddy never to love again, or would she continue on as if he had never existed? And what if her original man—the airman—managed to return home safe and sound? Would she marry him without thinking twice about Rip, whether or not he too managed to survive?

So many questions, yet so few answers.

The only thing he knew for sure was that he needed to see Deborah again. Because if their affair was meant to be short-lived, he needed to make certain he squeezed every ounce of life from it while he could. The thought of losing what he had only just gained sent Rip into another fit of short, jagged breaths. Shoot, not again.

Fresh air would help. The crisp, cool oxygen laced with morning dew, the singing larks, the constancy of the sun above, it all helped to put his mind at ease. Morning brought safety, comfort. Only the night, teeming with shadows of grim memories, held danger.

He ran along the sidewalks, making his way toward the cliff. He had been happy there yesterday evening; he could be happy there now—calm, relaxed, outfitted with the memories of Deborah, her infectious passion for life itself.

What he couldn't understand was why he'd already deemed their time together a memory, as if it had already ended, as if she had come to spend one perfect day with him than vanished forever. A swatch of purple on the horizon caught his eye, bringing with it the memory of Deborah twirling that plucked violet between her fingers as they talked. Its dark petals bringing out the purple undertones in her blue eyes, their softness mimicking the smoothness of her cheek.

He jogged over to the patch of wild grass and plucked the flower, then noticed a grouping of daisies farther out. He picked some of those too before journeying farther into the brush to gather black-eyed Susans, irises, even a few heart's delight. In hardly any time at all, he had a fine bouquet of beautiful wildflowers, every one of which sparked a comparison to Deborah in his mind's eye.

He couldn't wait another second to see her again, to prove she was still there, still interested in spending time with him. He stopped back at home to brush his teeth and hair, then headed to her home, so incredibly nervous he couldn't quite get a handle on himself.

"Coming!" a voice not unlike Deborah's called in response to his knock, and seconds later an aged version appeared in the doorway. "Yes. How may I help you?" She kept one hand on the doorframe and one on the knob, tense, ready to shut him out.

"I've brought these for Deborah." He managed a smile as he pushed the flowers toward the woman he assumed was Mrs. Walker.

"Oh, how sweet." Everything about the woman softened, revealing a striking similarity between her and her daughter. "But Deborah isn't home now. She's already left for her shift at the nursing home. Would you...would you like to come in for a glass of sweet tea?"

Before Rip could properly think her offer

through, Mrs. Walker had coaxed him into the dining room and served up a glass of tea with fresh mint. "Mind if I join you?"

"Please do," he replied, though he found it strange that she felt the need to ask in her own home.

"Now correct me if I'm mistaken, but didn't you just buy the Suttons' old place?" She sat down across from him and fussed over the pleats in her skirt.

"I rented it for a while."

She nodded and stared down her nose at him. "So you aren't planning on making this your home?"

"No, ma'am." He wondered if he should have said more, should have explained about the war, about questioning his place in it now that he'd met Deborah. But it was all so terribly complex, they'd have to make do with his simple response.

Mrs. Walker sighed and fixed her inquisitive gray eyes on him. "Please allow me to be blunt. What are your intentions for my daughter?"

It took everything Rip had to keep his breathing even. "We...Well, I—"

"You're a soldier, right? I'm assuming you're aware of her previous engagement with a boy in uniform. Of course, her father and I never met him, but she was smitten all the same."

She flung words at him quickly, too quickly for him to word a response. "I'm a Sergeant First Class," he answered at last.

"Retired? Home on leave? Discharged?" Each question hit him like a bullet.

Rip laced his fingers together and squeezed. The last thing he wanted to do was to have a nervous breakdown in front of this woman. "Temporary leave. Shell shock," he sputtered.

"Well."

"Well."

They both sipped at their tea, giving Rip enough time to plan what he should say next.

"My intentions are honest, ma'am. I like your daughter very much."

"She's been hurt, you know."

"I know."

"And she wouldn't be an easy wife to take, if a wife is what you're after."

He couldn't help but grin at the thought of Deborah as his Missus. "So far being around her is the easiest thing in the wide world," he admitted. "Besides, I've often discovered *easy* could just as well mean *boring*."

Mrs. Walker tapped her fingers on the tabletop and scrunched her features together as she appraised him. After a few more tense moments, a giant grin broke across her face. "You know what? I rather like you, young man. What's your name?"

"Rip Rockwell, ma'am, and I'd like your permission to take your daughter on a date tonight."

"Well, Rip, you've got it." She lifted her glass and stretched across the table to clink it on his. "She'll be home from her volunteer shift around four. Stop on by anytime after."

"Thank you. Nice meeting you, ma'am." Rip nodded in her direction and let himself out. He had five and a half hours to plan the perfect evening, and not a second to waste.

"Wear this," Mother said, thrusting a cherry-printed party dress Deborah's way the second she walked in the door.

"What for?"

Mother's eyes sparkled with mischief. "You have a gentleman caller this evening."

Deborah placed a hand on her hip and stared at her mother in annoyance. The last time she'd tried to fix up Deborah on a date, they had ended up so ill-suited that they hadn't even made it to the restaurant before calling it an evening.

"Now I know what you're thinking. I still maintain you and Harry would have made a lovely match, but that's not what this is about. A certain Sergeant First Class by the name of Rockwell stopped by this morning, and asked if it might be all right to take you out this evening."

Deborah couldn't hide her smile. "He did?"

"He did. A very nice young gentleman, so of course I agreed on your behalf."

"Did he say where he'd be taking me?"

"No, but he did leave these for you." Her mother motioned toward a bouquet of wildflowers resting in an etched glass vase on the counter.

Deborah wandered over to the kitchen and leaned down to smell the flowers' sweet fragrance. "Did he say when he'd be picking me up?"

"I told him anytime after four would be fine, which is why you need to get dressed. Now."

"Okay, okay." Deborah laughed. She liked that her mother seemed every bit as excited about this date as she was. They continued to talk as Deborah slipped into the dress and picked a simple pearl set from her jewelry box.

"You should take a cardigan too. It might get be

chilly tonight—and please let me do something with that hair of yours."

"Yes, Mother." Deborah finished getting dressed, then allowed her mother to powder her nose and curl her lashes.

"Mother, really. I'm sure Rip isn't expecting me to get all gussied up like this."

"That, my dear, is why you must. Gentlemen like to be kept guessing. It keeps them interested. Now pucker your lips, so I can apply a touch of pink."

Deborah rolled her eyes, but complied anyway. Partway into this impromptu beauty session, a knock sounded at the door.

"Stay here," Mother whispered. "I'll get it. Make him wait a little."

"Let me guess, gentlemen like that too?"

"Well, of course, they do. Now shush. You'll give us away."

Deborah chuckled to herself and listened as her mother's light footsteps crossed the house. A second later, she heard Rip's voice. "Good evening, ma'am. I'm here to pick up Deborah for our date."

"Well, c'mon in. Deborah's still getting ready, but you can wait with me and her father in the living room."

Deborah wondered how long she'd need to wait

in order to appease her mother's wishes. The whole ritual seemed silly to her, but she knew better than to disobey. Besides, she really didn't know the first thing about courtship, having only ever been on one prior date.

She ran through the lyrics of *Mona Lisa* in her head, imaging Rip's beautiful voice. When she reached the end, she decided she'd waited long enough and poor Rip had probably already been subjected to more than his fair share of her mother's merry badgering.

"I'm ready," she sang, walking out into the living room, a bit unsteady in the heels her mother had insisted upon.

Rip stood and kissed her on the cheek. "You look sensational."

She smiled coyly, doing her best to impress both Rip and her mother. "Are we ready to go?"

"Yes, indeed."

"Where are you taking our Deborah?" her father asked, coming over to clap Rip on the back.

"If you don't mind, sir, I'd really prefer to keep it a surprise."

Her father laughed, and Rip joined in nervously.

Eager for her surprise, Deborah took Rip's arm and tugged him toward the exit.

"Well, you two best be off," her mother chirped. "Have fun."

"And be home by ten," her father added. They clicked the door shut behind them.

"I've never met anyone's parents before," Rip confessed once they were seated in the cab of his truck together. "They seem nice."

"Thank you." Butterflies flitted within her chest. He'd met her parents and received their blessing. Her mother would no doubt want to hear everything about their date, and then it wouldn't be long before she started dropping little hints about marriage; after all, it had always been her dream for Deborah, to marry a nice, young man and to do so early, so she could have lots and lots of babies. She suspected the fact that she was an only child had not been by choice and often pitied her mother for this loss.

She looked out the window in silence as the truck pulled away from her house and onto the main road. "So now will you tell me where we're going?"

He grinned a Cheshire grin. "You'll find out soon enough, until then it has to be a surprise."

Deborah laughed. "You and your surprise."

"It will be worth the wait, I promise." He snuck a quick glance at her. His handsome face sent the butterflies into a tizzy once again.

About half an hour later, they pulled onto the busy streets of the big city. Deborah's mouth dropped open in awe as she took in the dizzying array of pedestrians, lights, and sky-high buildings. She hadn't been to the city for at least a year, and every time she managed to come back, it was as if the place had doubled both in size and population.

"We're here," Rip announced, parking across from a large concert hall.

"Now will you tell me?" she pleaded. Surprises were fun, but at the same time she'd prefer to know what they'd be getting into come evening.

He opened the door for her and offered her his arm. "I suppose now's a good a time as any. We're seeing a certain crooner on the big stage tonight."

"It isn't...?" Her throat constricted with excitement. She couldn't finish the sentence.

"None other than old King Cole himself."

Deborah squealed and wrapped her arms around Rip. "Oh, thank you. Thank you so much."

He beamed, then leaned in to whisper, "You know, I'd really like to kiss you right about now, but this is a very public place and I'd hate to embarrass you."

Deborah offered her cheek. "Until we can find

somewhere a bit more private," she teased, then tugged him by the hand toward the concert hall. As they got closer, she began to wonder where all the other show-goers had gotten to. Were she and Rip enormously early? Not even the ticket collector had shown up yet.

"I don't understand." Rip furrowed his brow. "The concert's supposed to start in half an hour."

"Let me see the tickets." Deborah waited as Rip fished the two folded admittance stubs from his wallet and studied them with consternation.

His lips moved as he read over the fine print on the tickets. "Oh, darn." He handed them to Deborah, a look of utter embarrassment plastered upon his face.

"The concert was yesterday. No wonder I got such a good deal on these." He groaned as he crumbled the tickets up and threw them in a nearby trash bin.

"Hey, never you mind now, you hear?" Deborah stroked his arm and smiled. "I wouldn't change how we spent yesterday evening for all the Nat King Coles in the world. Honest, I wouldn't."

And when Rip still didn't cheer, she decided to do away with propriety, pulled his face toward her own, and gave him a full, bedroom kiss. He kissed her back hungrily, also clearly having had enough of propriety and not enough of her mouth on his.

When they pulled apart, Deborah noticed a man wearing a janitor's uniform and pushing a broom across the sidewalk while staring in their direction. Maybe he'd been here last night too.

"Excuse me, sir." She grabbed Rip's hand and pulled him over to the stranger. "Nat King Cole, could you tell us where he's singing tonight?"

"Nah, ma'am. He was here last night."

"I understand. I'd like to find out where he went next on his tour. Could you tell us please?"

"*I* can't, but maybe this will help." He reached into the dust bin and pulled out an advertisement for Mr. Cole's tour across America. "That's him, innit?"

"Ah-ha!" she shouted, smoothing the paper in her hands and thrusting it toward Rip. "Austin at eight. That's not too far. We can still make the end of the show."

"But what about tickets?"

"The way I see it, we have at least an hour to figure that out. Let's scoot!"

"Thank you!" they called back to the man as they both ran to Rip's truck, holding hands. Seemed they were in store for an adventure or two that night.

CHAPTER 8

Austin presented an entirely different picture than the city they'd visited before. Here cars were parked everywhere pell-mell. Some had been pulled up onto the sidewalks in desperation to find a spot for the sold-out show.

While they drove, they'd hatched up increasingly hare-brained schemes as to how they'd get into the concert. But when they arrived, it only took Rip slipping the attendant a fiver. He wasn't sure whether he should feel relieved or cheated that their crazy plans to sneak in had been rendered moot.

Once inside, Deborah pushed her way through the crowd, never once letting go of Rip's hand. They ended up so close to the stage they could hardly believe it. Rip held tight to Deborah's waist as they swayed in time to the lyrical songs, and even sang right along with Nat on a few of his favorites. Being there amidst all the other writhing concertgoers, Rip felt emboldened, truly alive, and maybe even a little free—which he found rather funny considering all the bodies were packed together like sardines in a can. Having the prettiest girl in the entire state on his arm and knowing she was truly happy to accompany him lightened Rip's heart in a way nothing else had managed prior.

When the show came to a close, he and Deborah made their way back to his truck. She skipped like a schoolgirl, chattering away about how amazing the evening had been and thanking him profusely for planning the most perfect surprise anyone could ever imagine. "I would have liked for it never to end," she said. "That we could stand there, dancing side by side for all eternity."

Rip squeezed her hand and smiled. "I would have liked that too."

"Maybe it doesn't have to." She stopped walking, forcing the stream of foot traffic to divide in order to pass her.

"What do you mean?"

"I mean." Her eyes hinted at mischief. "That it doesn't have to be over."

He laughed and pulled on her arm to try to get her to move again. "Maybe it doesn't have to, but it has. Why else would everyone be headed to their cars?"

Deborah dug into her purse and pulled out the crumpled advertisement the janitor had given her.

"Let's see. Tomorrow he'll be in New Orleans. Oh, please say we can go!"

As much as he liked the idea of carrying their date into the next day as well, Rip also remembered... "Your father said to be home by ten. We're already going to miss your curfew by at least two hours."

Deborah blew a raspberry. "Oh, c'mon. We're already late, so what does it matter really? Tell you what, we'll call him from a payphone and explain. He'll have no choice but to agree."

The conflicting desires of remaining with Deborah and obeying her father's wishes battled it out, and ultimately his growing affection for the girl triumphed. "Okay," he said softly. Then louder, "Let's do it!"

Deborah cheered and pumped an unladylike fist in the air as they raced each other back to the truck.

"I can't believe we're doing this," he murmured while jamming the key into the ignition. "You sure bring out another side of me, Deborah."

"I wouldn't do it with anyone but you," she whispered sweetly and leaned in to plant a kiss on his cheek. "Now step on it!"

Deborah had shocked even herself by suggesting they follow Nat King Cole and his crew to the next venue, but she couldn't imagine saying goodnight to Rip and letting their magical evening come to an end. Oh, her father would be livid. She had no doubt about that, but she needed to do this for herself and for Rip too. At each of their meetings, he'd relaxed more and more into their time together, going from that brusque stranger glowering at her over a basket of muffins to the light-hearted suitor who accompanied her tonight.

She had bid her James goodnight once upon a time, and then had never seen him again. Part of her worried saying goodbye to Rip would also mean the end, and—well—she wasn't ready for things to be over. The concert, the courtship, the special feeling in her stomach whenever his lips brushed against hers.

"Oh, pull over here." She motioned toward a campground on their right. "We'll need some place to sleep for the night."

Rip frowned. "I don't think I have enough money for a motel."

She blushed. "That's okay. It wouldn't be proper for us to...anyway. I mean, we aren't...well, you know. Besides, this here truck is plenty comfy. Unless, I don't suppose, you have a tent hidden somewhere under here?" She rummaged through the emergency kit Rip kept stashed beneath the bench seat, but came up short.

"No, sorry."

"That's okay. We'll make do. After all, isn't that part of this adventure we're having together? C'mon, let's go for a walk." She pushed her door open before Rip had the opportunity to cross around the vehicle and assist in a display of gentlemanly behavior. Deborah wasn't much for tradition anyway, especially if it meant she had to sit and wait for help in opening a lousy door when she was plenty capable of taking charge on her own.

"Are we in Louisiana now?" she asked as they walked hand in hand down a dirt trail leading into a ravine.

"Only just. We crossed the state line a few miles back."

"I like it."

"Me too." He squeezed her hand as a twinkling display of lights flickered across the night sky.

"Wow," Deborah whispered. "It's like God just flipped on a switch."

"Or like the fireflies are in support of our romance." He stopped walking and put a hand on each side of Deborah's waist. "I am too. Rooting for us, I mean."

And they kissed. His mouth on hers was wet, searching. He hugged her tight to his body, and she could feel the growing desire as it struggled against his undergarments. He pulled back and searched her face, a smile tugging at the corner of each of his warm hazel eyes. The stars above shone down upon them as the fireflies continued their delicate dance across the horizon.

Suddenly a very strange feeling overtook Deborah. Not desire, not love, not any emotion she would have expected from such a romantic evening. Guilt and guilt alone gnawed at her gut, tore down the happy butterflies, so their wings no longer tickled her insides. She pulled away from Rip as if his skin was white hot.

"What's the matter?" he murmured, drawing close to comfort her.

James. James was the matter, but how could she tell him that? It was no fault of his she had pledged herself to another first. No fault of his that James had gone missing somewhere near the forty-first parallel and had stayed in that amorphous space, neither alive nor dead, for more than a year. What if he was still out there, a battered prisoner of war, clinging desperately to his life so he could make his way back to her? What if he were dead and she hadn't taken the time to properly mourn him before falling into the arms of another?

What if Rip returned to war and befell harm too?

What if? What if? What if?

The myriad possibilities danced through her mind, not one of them offering a happily ever after. Rip stared at her, his face a mask to whatever feelings he hid within.

"I'm just...very tired is all. Can we call it a night please?" Deborah stalked off toward the truck and let herself into the cab. And though her vexation continued, she eventually fell asleep nestled up against the cold car door. She'd much rather have been tucked safely in the arms of a man she was increasingly smitten with.

Why did everything need to be so complicated?

The next morning Deborah awoke to find herself wrapped in the very arms she had shunned the previous night. Rip slept serenely with a smile upon his face, breathing softly in time to the beat of her own heart. She carefully freed herself from his embrace and eased the car door open. The sun had begun to rise across the way, and she found herself walking swiftly in pursuit of the treeless horizon to get a better look.

Brilliant purples, oranges, and pinks took over the sky, and she watched, allowing the colors to take over her too. Deep breath in. Deep breath out.

Whether due to the sun's arrival or the good night's sleep, Deborah felt better in the light of day. Waking up in Rip's arms had felt right. Sleeping within them had also felt right, because she'd managed to slumber straight through the night, a feat she rarely managed even tucked into her own bed at home. And she couldn't remember making her way over to Rip's side of the cab. Seemed her subconscious knew precisely what to do, even if her waking mind was fraught with hesitation.

"I'm allowed to be happy," she told a curious bunny that had hopped across the path. "I'm allowed to carry on with my life."

The bunny sniffed at the air then continued on his way, and Deborah sighed. She willed her mind blank, tried to start over with her day. The sun continued to climb, dispersing its colors as it rose.

Suddenly, inspiration.

She hadn't brought her writing journal, so she

began to place words together in her mind. Yes, it would be the perfect way to set things right.

CHAPTER 9

Rip's body fell beneath the snow, deeper and deeper, its weight pinning him in place. Even though frigid air swirled around him, he felt uncontrollably hot, sweaty. The snow's moisture seeped into his clothes, his bones... *his mouth?*

His eyes shot open and he stared straight into the face of a beautiful woman, her body covered his, writhing as she continued to kiss him. And then it all returned to him—the concert, the campgrounds, Deborah's sudden change in disposition toward him. He was so dreadfully confused.

"Good morning, sleepy-head." She worked her fingers through his hair, pulling his face forward to meet her own. She'd flip-flopped on him again, but rather than fretting about it, he chose to relax and enjoy this surprise show of intimacy.

The topmost buttons on her dress had come undone, allowing him a glimpse of her breasts curving in toward each other, held back only by a sheer white fabric. Her nipples jutted out, firm, erect, and Rip felt his own privates follow suit. She must have felt it too, because she rocked back and pressed into him.

And they connected. Through three layers of clothing, but still, they connected—oh, how gloriously they connected.

He grew harder still and desperately wanted to unfasten the remaining buttons that shielded Deborah's supple, pale skin from view, wanted to lay her down on the soft grass outside and take everything she had to offer, a gift to cherish if ever there were one.

But it wasn't right, not like this. Deborah had so much more to offer than a beautiful face. Everything about her turned Rip on—his body, his mind, his heart—and he knew disrespecting her like this would be wrong, whether or not she seemed to want it too. Besides, hadn't she turned the cold shoulder on him last night?

"Are you hungry?" he asked, grasping at any change of topic he could find. But now that he mentioned it, his stomach did rumble, though certain other parts of his body were less difficult to ignore.

"Yeah, but..." She laughed and leaned forward to kiss him once again.

"Let's go find a nice little diner and get some flap-jacks and eggs. We have another long drive ahead of us today. We'll need our strength."

Deborah reluctantly climbed off his lap and slid to the passenger's side of the cab. Was she upset? Did she feel slighted? Whatever the case, she didn't let on. Maybe she, too, was relieved he'd put a stop to what they'd started.

"Are you looking forward to New Orleans?" he ventured.

"I am," she responded pertly. "But there's something else I'm looking forward to even more." She reached over and clasped his free hand in both of hers. "I have a surprise for you!" And there was that joy again, the same unbridled happiness she had shown when introducing him to the cliff.

"A surprise, huh? What it is?"

She laughed and wagged a finger in his direction. "Oh no, you kept your surprise until the bitter end. I get to keep mine too."

He chuckled along with her. "The bitter end? I would have thought you liked my surprise a bit more than that."

She playfully hit his arm, and—just like that—the brush-off she'd given him the night before receded to a distant memory.

Over breakfast, he asked, "Tell me about your work, where you go during the day."

And she told him about the nursing home and all its colorful residents, how she had started volunteering there at her father's insistence as a way to pass time over the summers, but had fallen so in love with it, she now assisted the staff full-time. She talked about the old folks who lived there, how each had such a vivid story to tell, how it really was a writer's paradise and one day she'd make sure to tell all their amazing stories for posterity.

"I never would have pictured myself at an old folks' home of all places," she admitted after taking a long gulp of orange juice. "But now that I'm there, I can't much picture myself anywhere else."

Rip poured more maple syrup over his pancakes and began to cut them into squares. He, for one, could picture Deborah in all kinds of places—his arms, his bed, his future—but he decided not to say anything so brazenly forward.

"What about you?" She picked up her fork and readied a bite of hash browns. "What do you do for work?"

"The Army," he answered bluntly.

She shook her head and put a hand over her mouth to cover the chewed up food inside. "No," she mumbled. "I mean, now that you're out of the Army. What will you do?"

"That's the thing, I'm not out. My leave is only temporary. I fully intend to go back and finish my term of service, to see my duty through."

"Oh, I see." She took another long swig from her juice cup. "Well, should we be off then?"

Rip agreed even though he hadn't eaten his fill yet. He hoped he hadn't ruined whatever this—amazing thing—was between them.

Deborah's mind and heart continued to war with one another as she and Rip finished their drive to New Orleans, enjoyed their concert, and then took the long drive home to their tiny Texas town.

Rip would leave, perhaps soon. He could die, he could disappear, he could forget about her. She'd never bought that ridiculous *absence makes the heart grow fonder* bit. In her experience, absence made the heart grow distant, cold. As it was, she could barely picture James's handsome face any longer, and it had hardly been more than a year since they last met. Since they'd first met too.

And she really didn't feel like being a war widow

twice over, but she also didn't want to let go of what she and Rip had, especially if everything turned out okay in the end, if the war ended before he could return, or if he came back unharmed and as in love with her as ever.

Of course, she didn't know exactly what Rip's heart held, but she knew hers—and she had fallen hopelessly, irrevocably in love. She'd known in that very moment when the fireflies danced their slow waltz through the night sky. She'd known, and it had terrified her. And had she not impulsively suggested they take this little road trip together, she'd have been able to feign illness, request to be taken home, to ignore Rip whenever he came calling for another date. But they had taken their trip, which meant her heart and her head had no choice but to battle it out as they drove across the country roads that led from one state to the next.

And now her time with Rip had amounted to approximately one hundred times more than what she'd ever had with James. And she freely admitted her love for him. So why couldn't she put her fears aside and give herself fully to Rip?

These questions continued to float about her mind as she and Rip pulled up to her house's darkened doorstep, as she gave him a quick kiss goodnight, and crept in through the front door. The tableside lamp in the living room snapped on, casting an elongated shadow across the floor.

There her father sat in his favorite armchair, a scowl set onto his normally friendly face. "Where have you been?" he rumbled.

Deborah froze, a deer in lamplight. "Daddy, I called from the payphone. I said I'd be—"

"*You said*? You *said*? What happened to *asking* permission first? Your mother and I would never have agreed to, to this overnight—" His voice stuck on *overnight*. "... affair."

"No, it wasn't like that. Nothing happened, I swear."

Just then, Deborah's mother padded into the room, her hair fixed in neat little rows of pink foam curlers. She yawned and wiped the residue from her eyes. "Deborah?" she croaked. "Do you have any idea how worried we've been?" She perched on the arm of her husband's chair and waited.

Deborah felt tears begin to well behind her eyes. "Mama, I'm so sorry. I didn't mean for you to worry. It's just we were having such a good time, and we— I...I wasn't thinking. But *nothing* improper happened between Rip and me, I promise."

Her father let out a low guttural sound, but her mother stood and took Deborah into her arms.

"If she says nothing happened, then nothing happened. But, Deborah..." She held Deborah at arm's length and looked straight into her eyes as she spoke. "This can *never* happen again, do you hear? It isn't proper for an unmarried woman to...well, you know."

"Yes, Mama."

Her father sighed but made no move to rise from his chair. "We're very disappointed in you."

"Yes, Daddy."

"And, of course, we will no longer allow you to see that, that, *boy* without a chaperone present."

Deborah nodded, though she didn't at all agree.

"Now go get some sleep."

Deborah fell into bed, allowing her tears to flow freely in the privacy of her own room. Yes, she was having a hard time deciding what to do about her affection toward Rip, but that didn't mean she wanted her father to make the decision for her. It hadn't been Rip's fault she'd insisted on staying out all evening and the next day too, hadn't been his fault they'd almost...In fact, he'd been the one to take a step back and slow things down like the true gentleman he'd proven himself to be. Not as if she could make *that* argument to her father.

With time, she fell asleep, memories of her grand adventure with Rip playing on loop within her dreams.

CHAPTER 10

Crash! Bang! Boom!

Angry chunks of shrapnel catapulted through the air. He tried to run, but he was stuck in place, lying on the ground with useless legs that refused to carry him to safety. George was down, and the enemy was drawing closer.

More blistering metal flew toward him. He watched helplessly as bits of the debris singed his shirt and melted into his chest.

The pain was like nothing he'd felt before and nothing he'd felt since—the sensation of a handful of fiery worms burrowing toward his heart, consuming him from the inside out. Hurt like heck.

He prayed for it to end once and for all, for his agony to cease. But the shrapnel and gunfire kept tearing through the sky, the pain kept progressing toward his heart.

Crash! Bang! Boom!

He struggled into a sitting position, and the pain fell away—but the sounds continued. Confused, Rip searched the dark room. *Home. Safe.*

Then what was all that ruckus?

He listened closely. The bangs gave way to gently *pings*. His window.

He rushed across the room and peered out into the nightscape. A cloaked figure ran forward, and for a moment terror groped his heart. The commies, they had found him. They had come to finish the job.

But, no, that didn't make any sense.

"Pssst!" a voice called, and then Deborah's mess of blond curls appeared on the other side of the glass.

Rip immediately pulled up the window and let the cool air rush into his room. "What are you doing here?" he asked, though he was ecstatic she had come.

"No time for questions. Come with me." She grabbed his hand and pulled him through the window. If she was surprised at his attire—pajama pants only—she didn't show it.

"Where are we going?" he asked, trying to keep up as she sprinted down the street.

"Your surprise, it's ready. And I wanted to give it to you right away."

He fell into step beside her, wracking his brain as to what the surprise may be. And moments later they'd arrived at the same lake where they had first become more intimately acquainted.

Deborah didn't hesitate. She pulled her nightgown right over her head, then stepped out of her undergarments as well. Her alabaster skin shone in the moonlight, and Rip wanted nothing more than to run over to her, take hold, and never, ever let go. But Deborah simply stretched her arms high over her head and ran giggling into the water.

"Come on in! The water's, well, cold, but you could help warm it up." He suspected a wink had accompanied her invitation, but couldn't be certain. Was Deborah's surprise...? No, it couldn't be.

He stepped out of his flannel pants, and a chill worked its way across his flesh. The scars on his chest reflected the moonlight just like her beautiful unblemished skin. He trotted into the water after Deborah, who had disappeared in the brief moment he had managed to tear his eyes away from her.

"Deborah?" he ventured, sweeping the lake in search of her.

A second later she popped up in front of him

and dragged him down beneath the surface. The moment they were both immersed, she brought her lips to his and pulled him tight to her breast. Only a brief sheen of lake water separated their naked bodies, and despite the odd setting, their odd predicament, being there with Deborah felt so *right*.

They broke into the air to pull some oxygen into their hungry lungs, then continued to kiss, to embrace, to take of each other.

And that was when he knew.

He needed to marry this girl so he could come home to her each and every evening, so he could wake from his nightmares in the comfort of her calming presence, so they could take their love to the next level, so he could, at last, be with her fully without worrying about disgracing her reputation or filling her belly with an unwanted child. Because he wanted it *all* with Deborah, the children, the picket fence, the whole shebang.

He pulled away from his beautiful lake goddess and swam back to shore. She followed close behind.

"That wasn't the surprise," she said.

He laughed. "No? I have a hard time imagining what could be better."

She slipped her nightgown back over her head

and motioned for him to join her on the grass. "Then let me show you."

He sat beside her and waited. For a moment, she seemed shy, but then he wrapped an arm around her and she turned to him with a smile.

With no preamble, Deborah began to recite the most beautiful words Rip had ever heard:

> "Once I was a lonely jailbird
> Not knowing I couldn't fly
> Then you chanced a smile my way
> And the whole world came alive
> Now that we're here together
> Everything feels so right
> And I feel compelled to tell you
> You are my guiding light
> Let me love you as you have loved me
> Because, darling, your love has set me
>   free."

She stopped and smiled a sad, sweet smile.

"I wanted to tell you how I feel, and it's always been easier for me to write it down first, so—"

He stopped her with a kiss. "Deborah."

"Yeah?" She glanced up at him from beneath wet lashes.

"I love you, too."

The crickets' chirps filled the early morning air, the only sound save for Deborah's and Rip's slow breaths as they sat in the wake of this giant admission.

She loved him. And he loved her back. It was that simple, and that enormously difficult.

"Did you like it? Did you like my poem?" she asked at last, jostling them from the serenity of the moment.

"I loved it." He squeezed her hand, a smile shooting across his handsome face. "Teach it to me. Let me turn it into a song, our song."

And so they sat together in the approaching dawn, Deborah saying a line, and Rip repeating it until he'd learned the entire thing. Then he was singing her own words back to her, sweet and melodic. She listened in awe as her words took on new life in Rip's mouth.

"Wow," she whispered when he'd finished. "That was so beautiful."

He raised his hand to her cheek and held her gaze, her heart, her everything. "Seems we're better together than either of us ever was apart," he said.

Deborah couldn't help but agree. How was it that love always crashed into her so suddenly and so wholly? Rip's eyes twinkled, reflecting the few remaining stars above, and she felt perfectly blissful wrapped in the faint morning light. Until...

"Marry me."

At first she couldn't be certain she'd heard him correctly. They'd only just declared their love for one another. Only made each other's acquaintance —what?—less than a week ago. But that couldn't be right. Another part of her felt she had known Rip all along or perhaps in another life, in a distant dream.

Then he said it again. "Marry me."

She watched the light leave his eyes, his strong form weaken as she answered, "Oh, Rip, I don't know."

Yet he persisted. "What's not to know? I love you. You love me. We're both young, our whole lives ahead of us. What could possibly be simpler? We belong together, Deborah. We belong together, you and me."

But what about James? Saying yes to Rip means saying goodbye to him forever, and I'm just not sure I'm ready to let him go, to admit he's...

She pulled away from him, stood, turned her

back, tried not to cry as she gave him her answer. "I —I'll have to think about it, about us. I'm sorry."

And then she ran away, ran home without even a second glance in his direction. All that was perfect faded away, and she was left only with an over- whelming sense of dread. For all the times she'd imagined receiving a marriage proposal, she'd never expected she'd want to say no every bit as much as she longed to say yes.

Chapter 11

Rip returned to his lonely suburban home more shaken up than ever. Nothing lasted. Not life, not happiness, not even home, he thought as he looked around the rented house that held so little of him within its walls.

What had he done to anger the Almighty so? Why did an unrelenting streak of misfortune follow him wherever he tried to hide? He always—always —tried to do what was just and good. He had tried to save George, he really had. He'd rejected Deborah's advances although he'd have liked very much to turn their affections physical.

He fell to the carpeted floor and hugged his

knees to his chest, rocking back and forth, back and forth, willing the motion to shake loose all the troubling thoughts from his mind. When that didn't work, he tried to take slow measured breaths, but they came out short as his throat constricted and he struggled to pull enough air into his tired lungs. The room spun around him, and he felt as though he were tumbling down an infinite spiral staircase.

Nothing was home. Nothing was safe. Nothing was good.

He needed to get back to the front lines, and soon. Because he'd already been used up, he'd already been broken inside. If he could take out a couple commies before going down, then perhaps he could save the life of another soldier, the life of some young buck with his entire life before him. Without Deborah, Rip's life had no meaning.

It had come to that now, hadn't it?

Deborah had managed to cure what the very best VA doctors could not. She had mended his broken heart, only to yank off the bandage that had held it all together, breaking him even worse than before. He pictured her face as she told him no, the fear in her eyes. He'd assumed she was lifting him up, but maybe *he* was pulling *her* down. He loved her; he had no doubt of that, so maybe it was best to let her go free—just as their song had stated: *Your love has set me free.*

Had she meant it as a way to brush him off? Had he been too dense to pick up on her intentions? Well, it seemed he had a choice. Now his love could set her free.

He hoped she could forgive him. Their affair had intensified much too quickly. He knew she was still in mourning for her lost airman. He *knew*, and still he pushed her to give it all, to give far more than she had left to offer.

He thought of Deborah, then George. He needed closure on both counts, oh how desperately he needed closure. Deborah had helped him make peace with George's memory, but losing her now brought back every bit of pain he'd managed to suppress over the last several days, all at once —*whoosh*—in a torrent.

And he was drowning in it. Drowning. When the air began to come more regularly, he pressed his uniform, got dressed, and started up his truck. The Army had to take him back, seeing as he no longer had anywhere else to go. Korea was calling once more, and he planned to answer.

Deborah tiptoed into her house for the second time that night, although morning had almost reached their cozy little suburb by the time she found her way back home. She breathed a sigh of relief when the living room revealed no angry father, no disappointed mother, no lamp clicking on.

Slowly, she wedged open the door to her bedroom, and inside lay her mother fast asleep on the bed. *Drat*!

Well, she could face her mother now, or she could wait and face both her parents together. Best to be over with it, she supposed.

"Mother, I'm here," she whispered, nudging her mother's shoulder while kneeling near the bed.

"D-Deborah?" Her eyes blinked open and she smiled. "There you are."

"Yes, here I am." She waited for her mother's face to freeze over, for the lecture to begin. Only it didn't.

"You were out with the Sergeant again." A statement, not a question.

Deborah nodded.

"And you've fallen quite hard for him."

Another nod.

"Well, what are you going to do about it?"

The past year swirled through Deborah's mind; memories blurred together. She saw James for the first time at the soda fountain, Rip standing in the door frame. She remembered kissing James under Huxtable's watchful gaze, and Rip in the waters beneath the cliff. Love, fear, not knowing what came next.

"I don't know, Mama."

"Then it seems you have some thinking to do." Her mother stretched and sat up in bed, pulling Deborah's curly head into her chest and stroking her hair.

Deborah debated telling her about his admission of love, about his proposal, but felt it better to keep the finer points to herself until she actually figured out how she wanted to answer Rip's request.

"Mother?" she whispered.

"Yes, dear."

"How did you know father was the one?"

"Trying to choose between the one we never met and the one we just met, are you?" Instead of waiting for a reply, her mother chortled softly. "I reckon it's because he's the only one who ever asked."

"Oh." Deborah tensed. That hadn't been the answer she was looking for. She'd loved and been loved by two men. Opening the door to one would mean forever saying goodbye to the other, and turning her back on love seemed like a very difficult thing to go.

"But," her mother continued. "I didn't need anyone else to ask. I knew straight away I'd be his girl." She chuckled again. "Well, maybe not *straight* away. I actually despised him at first, but it didn't take long for the daggers I shot in his direction to turn to daffodils. And when he asked me to accompany him for a walk about town, I couldn't help but agree."

Deborah thought back to her first meeting with Rip, the one in which he had been so rude. Then she thought of James asking her to spend his last night with him. Which man should she pledge her love to? Surely, she couldn't pick both, and choosing neither saddened her to the point of despair.

"Don't worry," her mother said, apparently sensing her confusion. "You'll figure things out in time. And probably not even as much time as you think." She gave Deborah a kiss on top of her head, then stood to leave the room.

"I'll leave you with this: try to picture your life without each of them. The one you can't imagine saying good-bye to is probably the one who's meant for you. Good luck, dear."

Deborah lay down on top of her quilt and did

and did as her mother had suggested. She thought of James and their perfect romance, of Rip and their whirlwind affair. She pictured saying goodbye and losing them both forever. And as a tear crept down her cheek, she knew exactly what she needed to do.

Chapter 12

Deep breath in. Deep breath out. Cough.

"Well, everything sounds in working order. How is the shell shock treating you these days?" the doctor asked, while pressing his cold stethoscope against Rip's chest.

"Oh, I'm just swell." Rip smiled to prove it.

The doctor frowned. "No more nightmares? No more waking up in a cold sweat?"

"No, sir. I'm ready to get back to the action. Seems the brief time away helped me to heal. Now I'm ready to honor the commitment I made to this country."

He studied Rip's chart through wire-framed glasses. "Everything seems good. I'll just need to run a few more tests, but if everything turns out as I suspect, you'll be cleared to return to duty. They say there's a new Asian conflict brewing. They'll need experienced NCOs such as yourself to show the green kids over there how to fight. One way or another, there's enough commies to go around. Are you up for the challenge, Sergeant?"

"Sir, yes, sir!"

"Then it seems you've got our work cut out for us. Go on and head home. I'll give you a call later today to confirm your results."

Rip hadn't expected bluffing the medic to come so easily, but he also hadn't expected to become so desperate to return to Korea, or somewhere else in Asia, or anywhere but that small suburb that held all his best memories with Deborah. Somehow somewhere he could finally be of use. Whether that meant living to fight another day or dying the moment he stepped foot on international soil, well, he wasn't sure he even cared all that much. He'd just head home, pack his bags, return to base, and await further instructions from his commanding officer.

The moment Deborah's shift at the nursing home ended she raced toward Rip's house to give him her answer. Yes, yes, as many yeses as there were fireflies in the sky on that dark Louisiana night when she had known for sure that they fit just right in each other's arms. She'd been scared then, and she was scared now. But hadn't Roosevelt once said something about the scariest thing in the world being none other than fear itself?

Being afraid meant she had something to lose, and that something was Rip, the one true love of her life. Could things have worked out with James in another life? Surely they could have, but she'd already been living without him for the past year, and somehow she'd managed to survive. She wasn't certain she'd be able to do the same with Rip, were she to turn his affections away.

Yes, she had decided, and she couldn't wait to tell the whole world, starting with Rip himself. She threw her bike onto the lawn and raced to his front door, so excited she practically shook with anticipation.

Knock, knock.

She pictured him opening the door and throwing his arms around her, lifting her up and spinning her about in circles. She pictured the kiss they would share, the look of pure joy that would blossom on her mother's face when they told her the good news.

When no one answered, she knocked again.

Sleeping, he was probably sleeping. After all, neither of them had gotten much if any sleep the previous night.

She knocked a third time, and finally a haggard, old woman opened the door. It took her a moment to recognize the woman standing before her. "M-Mrs. Sutton, hello. How are you today?"

Cold fingers of dread clenched at Deborah's heart. Where was her fiancé? Where was the man she loved?

As if reading her mind, Mrs. Sutton said, "Looking for the soldier boy? I'm afraid he's left, and in quite a rush too. He left me some mess to clean up before this place will be rentable again."

Deborah had to force the words out. "I don't understand. Why would he leave?"

"Going back to the front lines from what I hear. Says he's all fixed in the head and ready to move on with his life." Her voice softened and she cast an expression of pity toward Deborah. "Why, darlin', you knew this was only temporary, didn't you?"

She sighed and pulled Deborah to her bosom. "Oh, honey."

Deborah sniffed and pried herself from the old woman's grasp. "I-I have to go."

And just like that she was off, running back to

her house, grabbing her father's car keys from the little ceramic dish next to the door, and embarking on the long drive to the airport. Maybe it wasn't too late. Maybe she could catch Rip before he left once and for all.

Oh, this was all her fault. She should've said yes the moment he asked, or at least not have run away. Because now he was following suit, running so far away it would be impossible for her to follow. That is, unless she managed to catch him first.

She pulled into the airport's bustling parking lot, leaving her father's car at the curb. She'd be in so much trouble when it got towed, but she'd be in even more trouble if she just narrowly missed Rip by taking the time to find a proper parking space.

Inside the terminal, she spied a young woman kissing her beau goodbye. They embraced, then he hiked his duffel over his shoulder, pulled his cap down over his eyes and strolled through the gate. The airport attendant shut the door behind him and returned to her desk.

Deborah ran over to her. "Where is this flight headed?" she begged as she pressed her sweaty palms into the counter.

"Vietnam, ma'am, but we're all full up."

"Please, can I just have a moment to speak with one of the passengers?"

"I'm sorry, ma'am, no. We've already closed the gate."

"But you don't understand," Deborah cried, turning so the stranger wouldn't see her sob. She watched as the plane rolled across the terminal, then picked up speed and lifted from the ground, taking with it any last hopes she had of securing her very own happily ever after.

No college, no husband, and no happiness. She'd probably live with her parents all her life, volunteering at the nursing home, watching all her closest friends die off one by one, only to be replaced by a new batch of seniors who would soon die as well.

Bleak.

Someone came up behind her and placed a hand on her heaving shoulder. She sucked back her tears and readied an explanation for the attendant. Only...

Rip.

She grabbed onto him and held him tight, searching his eyes for an answer. "I thought you had left."

"I was going to. But turns out the doc said I wasn't cleared for combat anymore. Something wrong with my heart." He tapped on his chest, the same place where all the silver scars lay hidden beneath his uniform.

She placed her hand over his and vowed never to let go of what they had again, not even for a moment. She kissed him, and said, "Well, maybe I can help with that. If you'll still have me."

Rip's handsome smile broke across his face. "I'd very much like that."

LOOK HOMEWARD, ANGEL

The call came on the warmest day of summer, which was ironic really, since the news meant he'd be moving to the coldest part of the country.

"Alaska?" Deborah wrinkled her nose when he told her, and he immediately regretted even considering leading his new wife so far away from her family.

But then her features softened, and a huge grin stretched from cheek to cheek. "Oh, I've always wanted to go to Alaska! Do you think we'll see penguins?"

Although Rip knew for a fact penguins lived at the South Pole and not the North, now hardly felt the time to quibble over minor details. He took his bride in his arms and studied her carefully. Deborah always wore her emotions plain as day across her face. The only answer he needed to make this decision was the look in her eyes, and that look was...

Full of love and nothing else.

"I know what you're doing." She laughed. "Yes, let's move to Anchorage. It will be like an adventure."

"You're really sure?" he asked once more. "I could get a job here in Texas. We could stay near your family."

She planted her hands on either side of his neck and brought her forehead close to his. "*You* are my home. Not Texas. Not Alaska. Not any*where*. Wherever we can be together, that's where I'll be happiest." She smiled, and her tone became playful. "Besides, the Army is such an important part of who you are, and this Cold Weather and Mountain Warfare program thingy sounds perfect. Maybe I can take up knitting. Seems we'll need lots of extra thick socks where we're headed."

And by January of the next year, they found themselves living in a tiny apartment just a few miles removed from the base of Fort Richardson.

Alaska proved itself to be every bit as cold as Texas had been hot.

"Look at that moose!" Deborah shouted as they drove the last few miles in their several day journey to this strange, new home. "He's just walking across the road without a care in the world. Can you believe that? Hey, Mr. Moose, where you headed?"

She collapsed back into her seat in a fit of giggles. "Oh, Rip. Isn't it just as you'd imagined it would be? It's like a winter fairy land. I half expect Santa to show up with his reindeer and welcome us to the neighborhood."

Rip smiled and bobbed his head. While his wife was charmed by their surroundings, Rip felt fear clench hold of his heart.

The ice, the snow, the below-zero wind chill, it all brought back the memories he'd tried so hard to forget. Freeze-locked guns, enemy fire raining from the skies, blood seeping out from fallen soldiers staining the snow red...

There would be no rest for him. Each night starting with the first in their new home, he'd wake up screaming. Deborah did her best to comfort him by offering a warm glass of warm milk and stroking his hair until he fell back to sleep, but the night terrors persisted.

Night after night, he watched his friend George fall before him; he tried to work the ice out of his legs, to run, but he was stuck in place as the bullets flew toward him. Any second now, he'd...

He woke up gasping for breath.

"Hush, hush," his wife said from across the room. Suddenly, the overhead light flickered to life, revealing the starkly decorated room they had yet to make their own.

"What time is it?" he asked.

"It's five in the morning." She returned to his side, sat down next to him, kissed his forehead. "Take the day off, spend time with me," she urged. "We'll take a long weekend."

He hesitated, but Deborah was quick to justify her request.

"I think it's time we saw just how many good memories are here too. Let's have an adventure, Rip. After all, we're a bit overdue for something fun."

The way she smiled with such earnestness as she awaited his answer was more than enough to convince him of her plan, but before they could get started, Rip had a plan or two of his own... He pulled Deborah back into bed kissing her with an urgency he so often had when it came to his beautiful bride.

"Well, *this* is certainly fun." She giggled as he

helped her out of her pajamas and into his arms. They made love quietly, then slipped off into the predawn light to begin their next great adventure.

Deborah had been ready for this. She knew living once more among the snow and mountains would trigger Rip's shell shock, but she also knew they could get through it together. That's why she'd spent so much time in the library and on the phone with various travel agents prior to their big move—and she'd done it all in secret, of course.

Now the long weekend was stretched before them, and she knew exactly how she wanted to spend it. The timing couldn't have been more perfect, either.

"Where to?" Rip said as the engine of his truck rumbled to life.

"That's the best part." She knew if she showed her excitement, he would soon follow suit. "We're taking the long road to Fairbanks!"

Rip shot her a quizzical expression, but she was not to be deterred.

"Don't worry, it will be fun, and fun is just what

we need right now. I have it all planned out. It will be lovely, I promise."

He leaned in to kiss her on the cheek, then pulled out onto the main road. Sometimes they needed words to communicate; at other times, just a glance said the world. Today she felt the words of another would suit them best. She fiddled with the knob for the radio. Luckily, it only took a few moments to find exactly what she had been looking for.

Nat King Cole's smooth, angelic voice danced across the airwaves and into the cab of their truck.

Rip smiled and swayed to the beat.

When the chorus arrived, Deborah belted it out loud and spirited and completely off key.

"Oh, my lovely, little lark whose song is sweet only to me." He laughed, and Deborah jabbed him in the arm but then joined in.

"Sing it for me, Rip. Just like you did that first night, lying out by the cliffs as the sun dried our clothes. Don't you remember?"

He reached across the seat to hold her hand. "And then that second night when we arrived for his concert only to find we'd missed it by a day. I thought you were crazy when you suggested we drive to the next venue."

"Don't forget the one after that too!" She squeezed his hand. "You needed a little crazy in your life. Still do as a matter of fact."

"Always will. Forever." He took his eyes off the road for a moment, took her in, then began to sing in his strong, beautiful voice that easily rivaled that of their favorite singer.

The drive went by quickly as they listened to the radio, shared their favorite memories, and flirted the way only newlyweds so drunk with love can. It was past noon when they reached their destination in Fairbanks. After a late breakfast at a small diner very much reminiscent of the ones they'd frequented back home in Texas, they made their way to the Chena Hot Springs.

If someone had told Deborah she'd be donning her bathing suit in thirty-below weather, she'd have told them they were crazy. Yet here they were, preparing for a relaxing soak in the exposed winter air. But that wasn't all she had planned for them...

"Remember the night you proposed to me?" she asked.

"And you ran away?" He laughed, then looped an arm around her shoulders and pulled her in tight to his chest. "Sorry, not my best memory."

His slippery skin felt so good against her own,

making her even more excited about what she planned to suggest.

"Hey, I came back! I said yes! But before then, when we..." Her eyes darted toward the water below.

"Oh no, Deborah. You couldn't possibly—!"

His protest was cut short when she slipped her shoulders under the water and eased out of her swimming costume. She handed it to him in a tight ball. "Your turn," she whispered.

As the day marched on, Rip felt the grip of his shell shock ease loose. If ever there were a cure for what ailed him, his sweet, kooky wife was it. Didn't matter the ailment, either. Deborah was good for his soul, plain and simple.

He often wished he could be as devil-may-care as she, and, much to his surprise, found himself getting closer and closer to joining her there. She'd suggested the naked dip, but it was he who'd found the isolated spring where they could make love within the ancient waters.

The day passed far too quickly, but then again, every day with Deborah did. Luckily, they still had forever stretched out before them.

Her eyes glinted with thinly veiled mischief as they surveyed the surrounding mountains. She pointed to a vast lake on the horizon. "Remember cliff diving? We should go—"

"No."

"You didn't let me finish," she pouted.

He sniggered and motioned for her to continue.

"We should go cliff diving next. What do you say?"

He laughed even louder. "Exactly what I was going to say earlier. If we dive now, we'll both break our necks. The lakes are ice this time of year!"

She blew a raspberry. "A technicality!"

Rip drew Deborah into his arms and kissed her forehead. "What else do you have planned for us?"

"Well, I can't exactly say it the right way, so I'm going to spell it once, and then you just have to accept that I'm going to mispronounce it, okay?"

He kissed her again, pulling her to him, and feeling his desire surge for a third time that day.

Deborah bit his lip playfully then pulled away. "Hey, don't distract me. It's hard enough to spell, let alone say. We're going to take a nice hike and see the I-N-U-K-S-U-K-S. Or as I prefer to call them, the In-nuk-nuks."

"The In... nuk-nuks?"

"Precisely! C'mon, I'll show you what I mean."

They returned to the fitting rooms and put on their long underwear and warm sweaters once more.

"It isn't far from here," she said. "Take my hand. We'll walk it."

"So the inuksuks," Rip said, figuring out the pronunciation of the strange Inuit word.

Deborah shook her head. "No, I told you, we're going to call them the in-nuk-nuks, because I can't say it the other way, and I don't want to feel silly all by myself."

He laughed, just as he always did when Deborah was near. "Okay, the in-nuk-nuks."

She nodded. "Good. Continue."

"What are they?"

"They're kind of like little baby Stone Henges. Do you remember studying Stone Henge in school? These are the ones the Eskimos make. They're a bit shorter, but there are so many more. Look!" She pointed in the distance. "See it?"

"Ahh, yes. Neat. What were they built for?"

"All kinds of reasons, really, but my favorite is as landmarks. They were built to show you the way."

They stood for a moment, two small figures amongst the vast, imposing winter landscape.

"Wait there," Deborah instructed, placing a hand

on each of his shoulders and pushing down to root him in place. "And close your eyes."

He did as he'd been told, remembering their cliff dive once again. He'd obeyed, but had still found a way to chance a peek at her exposed form in all its untouched glory. Now he listened as her feet slapped across the field.

When at last she spoke again, her voice sounded very far away. "Okay, open up!"

She stood beside the inuksuk with a hand on one of its many stones.

He smiled and began to jog toward her, but she waggled her finger wildly at him.

"Not so fast! Stay right where you are, and I mean it!" When she saw that he'd complied, she continued. "Like I said, the in-nuk-nuks were built to show you the way. And, Rip, darling, I know sometimes it's hard to let go of the past, especially when there's so much you regret, but as I tried to show you today, the past is also chock full of beautiful memories too. And all those memories, both terrifying and terrific, are gone. We've already lived them. Listen to the in-nuk-nuks. They know where to go." She opened her arms wide, inviting him in. "Come to this guide post. Come to me, to our future together as lovers, as husband and wife, and as... parents."

He couldn't move, though it was not for ice encroaching upon him, but rather, a creeping warmth that started at his heart and flowed outward. "What did you say?" he asked, just to be sure.

"Rip..."

He could see her eyes sparkling with the beginnings of tears, felt the same joy prick at his own eyes.

"We're going to have a baby."

And he was off. Never had his legs moved as fast as they did on that day to bring him to his wife and their child within her—his entire future in one neat, little package with blonde, curly hair and the world's most gorgeous smile. They stood there embracing for a long time, whispering declarations of love, stating their dreams for the future, and just basking in the grandness of being together.

At last the northern lights joined them, glowing green and proud against the night sky and marking a beautiful new chapter of their lives, one Rip couldn't wait for them to experience together.

Always together.

I'LL NEVER STOP
LOVING YOU

CHAPTER 1

Green had never been Rico's color. Yet, here he was dressed in it head to toe, ready to fight and die by a color that had never done him any favors—for a country that had let him down every bit as much.

"Don't go," Gloria whispered in her brother's ear so as not to upset their younger siblings. "You don't have to go."

His eyes searched hers and he spoke softly. "But, *mi hermana*, don't you understand? If I do this, things could change for all of us. It's just a couple years of my life. Then all our lives will be better. We could be citizens, Gloria. Think of how much easier things will be then."

She forced a smile. Rico had always been too optimistic for his own good. Didn't he know he could die cold and alone halfway across the world? And for what? The chance that maybe *maybe*— because it wasn't even a full-fledged promise—they could become citizens of a country that would still discriminate against them for their tan skin and south-of-the-border accents?

Still, Rico needed her support now. He'd already made up his mind, and the last thing he needed was to be distracted on the battlefield by any lingering worries. He needed to fight hard and come home alive and free. Who was she to say the government wouldn't deliver upon its hints at citizenship?

"Come back safe, Ricardo." Somehow using his full name felt like offering a blessing. She squeezed him tightly, then watched as he turned and walked into the admin building and out of his family's sight.

Her younger brothers stood silently—a rare sight —while her mother murmured a *Hail Mary* under her breath and clutched at her rosary like a security blanket. Papa couldn't take the time off work, not even to bid his son farewell.

They stood and stared at the closed door for

what felt like a very long time. Finally Gloria wrapped an arm around her mother's shoulders and said, "Come, Mama, let's get you out of this cold."

It didn't matter that the temperatures were in the high seventies or that somehow the simple, closed door made them all feel closer to Rico. The exertion of this outing had already begun to take its toll on her ailing mother. The prayers now came out raspy with long pauses in between each line as she struggled to catch her breath.

Gloria offered one herself and tried not to think about everything that could go wrong for Rico, for Mama, for all of them.

Oh, what would she ever do without her brother?

Everything about his new quarters felt different. Sure, it was set to Air Force regulations. The furniture—if you could call it that—looked the same, the walls were the same boring shade of egg white, but still it *felt* different. The air smelled of tobacco mixed with soggy plant life, and boy, was it humid. The sun didn't shine quite as bright either, as if it too knew there was a war on and didn't want to fully open its eyes to see the carnage.

But things wouldn't be so bad.

He told himself he'd become an airman because of his love of flying. But, truth be told, an even larger part of him wanted to avoid the realness of up-close combat. Dropping bombs from a safe distance, he could do—but looking into the bloodshot, sleep-deprived eyes of the enemy as he gunned him down across the field? No, he was far too afraid of what he'd learn about the enemy, about his fellow soldiers, and—most of all—about himself.

All that would start tomorrow. Tonight, he only had to find a way to get some sleep in this strange new place. A place he'd either be leaving as a deco-rated hero or as stuffing for a body bag.

James sank onto the thin plastic mattress. The springs sighed beneath his weight, but otherwise held steady.

"You ready to go get them commies?" Tommy Morrison, his friend from back home, asked as he scribbled away at a notebook in his lap.

"Ready as I'll ever be, I suppose. What you got there?"

Tommy held up the notebook and flipped

through a few pages. "Letter to Diana. I want her to know we arrived all right."

James grinned. "You're going to marry that girl, aren't you?"

"Soon as we secure victory." He tore a couple pages from the spiral pad and handed them to James. "Here. May as well write your girl a letter, too. Deborah, is it?"

He accepted the pages and grabbed a pen from his pack. "Thanks. Just my luck to find the perfect girl the night before deployment, isn't it? Think she'll wait for me?"

"Who'd wait for a buffoon like you?" Tommy laughed as he continued to scribble away at his notebook. "Nah, you know I'm only giving you a hard time. Of course, she'll wait, Jimmy."

James smiled as he pictured Deborah running into his arms at the airport the moment he arrived back on U.S. soil, her blond curls bouncing as she shook her head with laughter, her cherry lips eagerly searching him out, saddling him with a whole battalion of long-awaited kisses.

But what could he say to her now? He didn't want to write unless he found something romantic, profound, or, heck, even informative to say. However, words did not come easy as the nib of his ink pin floated hopefully above the blank page.

Why was this so difficult?

He ran his fingers up and down the sides of his bed as he thought. The cool metal framing beneath his mattress felt good against his warm skin. Suddenly, his hand snagged on something decidedly not metal.

"Tommy, I think there's something under here." James said as he stooped down on the floor and lifted the mattress for a better look.

"Ah-ha." He quickly found the tattered picture one of the previous residents had, no doubt, left behind and showed it to his bunkmate.

"Pretty. Who do you think she is?" Tommy tossed the photo back to James.

"Careful, would ya?" James took a moment to study the large walnut shaped eyes, the full lips, and dark hair of the exotic beauty in the photo. "Maybe somebody's girl back home, but why would he leave it here?"

"I reckon it wasn't on purpose. He probably..."

"Yeah." A moment of silence passed between them as they both thought of what had likely happened to the photo's previous owner. What could very well happen to either of them.

After a few beats, James broke the far-too-serious silence. "I think I'll hang on to this," he announced, tucking the photo into his pack. "A lucky charm."

"Suit yourself." Tommy set his pen to the page once again, tuning his friend out.

James leaned back on the mattress and put his arms behind his head. While the discovery of the photo had been exciting, he still had no idea what he was going to write to Deborah. Maybe things would come clearer in the morning.

With time he drifted off to sleep. Dreams, not of his sweetheart all the way back home, but of the mysterious beauty from the photo, greeted him as he slumbered in the strange bunk.

CHAPTER 2

Gloria patted her hands with flour and rolled out a fresh tortilla while her younger brothers ran around the room playing cowboys and Indians. Papa had left for work before the sun had risen, and Mama, who wasn't feeling good, had taken to resting in the back room. That meant it was up to her to make the meals for the day and take care of the house before heading off to her shift at the factory. Life was never boring; that much was for certain.

She dropped the circular swatch of dough onto the skillet and rolled out another as she waited for it to cook. Humming to herself helped the work go by faster and made her obligations enjoyable rather than a burden.

"Gloria, Gloria!" Her brothers came tearing into the kitchen, drawing dangerously near to the open flame on the stove.

"Be more careful, you hear me? You'll catch fire."

They broke into chuckles, but her youngest brother Pablo seemed troubled. He pulled at the seam of her shirt while the other two boys returned to their game of pretend.

"Yes, what is it?" she asked as she continued her work at the counter.

"Somebody's at the door. I looked through the window, and it's a man wearing a uniform like the one Ricardo had." Having delivered his news, the boy chased after his brothers, rejoining in their laughter.

But for Gloria it was as if all the air had suddenly been sucked out of the room. Although she inhaled and exhaled, oxygen wasn't making it into her lungs. She leaned back against the counter to steady herself and then slowly made her way over to the doorway.

This time she heard the doorbell as it sounded again.

"Be right there," she called. She dusted her hands off on the lap of her apron then pulled hesitantly at the knob.

And just as Pablo had described, a man wearing a dress uniform stood on the front step, a folded flag tucked into the crook of his arm, a grim expression on his face.

She didn't need to welcome the soldier inside, didn't need to ask how she could help him, but she did anyway.

The man took his cap off as he entered, then handed her a document. "Ricardo Flores the Third fought bravely and died for his country," he said.

Gloria scanned the document announcing the known details of Rico's death and fought back the urge to tell the soldier this wasn't *his* country, neither he nor their parents had been born on U.S. soil.

"He was wounded in battle," the officer continued. "Died before we could get him to the medic. I'm so sorry for your loss." He rocked on his feet from heel to toe, his hands clasped behind his back. And suddenly Gloria felt every bit as sorry for this stranger as she did for herself. How many families had he shattered with such news during the tenure of his duty? Did it ever get any easier? She spied a trace of sorrow knitted into his brow, which told her all she needed to know.

"Thank you, Sir." She guided him to the door and bade him goodbye. Now it was her turn to become the messenger.

Mama and Papa will be so sad, she thought. They truly hadn't seen this coming. They'd believed Rico's rosy view of the future, hadn't even considered...

Pablo toddled over and buried his small face in her lap. His sobs, even while muffled by her apron, proved deafening. Somehow the little boy's tears confirmed the soldier's announcement, made it true that they had actually lost their eldest brother.

She knelt down and hugged him, allowing her own tears to fall. Soon her other brothers joined them in a small huddle right on the living room floor, united by the loss, their number forever down by one.

Gloria wondered if she'd ever feel whole again.

They'd put him on search and rescue along with nine other men. Tommy wasn't one of them. James took a moment to admire the nose art of the SB-29 Superfortress they called the Saving Grace. He shot a wink at the sexy pinup of a naughty nurse before hopping in and bracing himself for takeoff. He wouldn't be the one flying this beautiful hunk of metal. Not today anyway.

As the monoplane soared over the land, James couldn't help but appreciate the rolling tranquility of the clouds that hung over the war zone—such beauty over such destruction. How was that for irony? But he couldn't allow himself to get hung up on the scenery. He needed to scour the terrain below in search of the platoon that had gone missing a few days prior.

"Those yellow-bellied commies sure know how to hide," another airman said with a Southern drawl. "Makes me wonder if they can fight."

"I only hope we never find out," someone else said.

"I think I see something," James whispered as if the enemy were close enough to overhear. "Take another pass."

As they drew closer to the source of his interest, James squinted, trying to make out the regalia on the distant men's uniforms. Was this the batch of missing soldiers or just another enemy outcropping? Before he could get a closer look, a terrible boom shook their plane.

"What the...!" someone cried.

Another wracking boom, and the engines fell deathly silent. The pilot wrestled with the controls, fighting to keep their fifty-ton bird airborne for as long as possible.

James mumbled a quick prayer under his breath. Somehow hoping the single word "please" would be enough to protect the lives of the men below, of his crewmates, and, of course, of himself.

The only sense he had left was sound. He didn't feel the pain of impact, or smell the singed metal as it crashed into the ground, but, oh, could he hear the screams of his fellow airmen.

"Tell Sally I love her," one said.

"Nooooo," another cried.

Mangled cries arose as some men died and others watched their blood squirt from gaping wounds. Bones popped from flesh.

James squeezed his eyes shut, hoping if he didn't look, none of it would be true.

Perhaps he lost consciousness, or perhaps they were ready and lying in wait. Because the next thing he knew, a pair of men had yanked him from the wreckage and prodded him with their rifles.

His eyes flitted open and took in the strange, small men. How could such diminutive people take down their powerful war machine?

They spoke loudly in a language he didn't understand. It wasn't clear whether their words were meant for him or for each other, but it *was* clear they were agitated. They pulled him to his feet, forced his head down, and led him away from the Superfortress. He didn't have time to see if any of the other men had survived. He couldn't see where his captors were taking him.

All he had left was the mismatched symphony that boomed around him and—he hoped—the photo he had found the night before. His lucky charm, he'd said. Well, he'd be needing every last scrap of luck he could find if he were ever to make it out of this strange land alive—let alone a hero.

CHAPTER 3

Gloria sat alone in the room she had always shared with Rico, although normally it had been divided by a curtain to give each a small measure of privacy. She sifted through his belongings to determine what to keep, what to donate, and what to throw away. Of course, Mama was no help. Instead she'd taken a vow of silence hoping it would help Rico reach heaven a little faster. This meant she kept herself sequestered in her room even more than usual, intermittently napping and coughing her phlegm into a cloth napkin.

Gloria checked on her often, and mostly allowed her younger brothers to fend for themselves. Eating cold leftovers for a day wouldn't harm them any. Besides, the faster she finished this work, the faster all these constant reminders of what she had lost would be gone.

Now her next oldest brother, Hector, had taken over Rico's side of the room. She hated how quickly life moved on for the rest of them when it had come crashing to a sudden and permanent halt for her favorite brother and oldest friend.

When she went to bed at night, she stared up at the mural Rico had painted above their beds, a colorful night sky hardly visible by the light of the moon glowing through the window. He had wanted to be an artist, but knew such a luxury was never to be. Not when he—like she—had to help support the family.

What would she do if she were completely free to pursue her own ambitions? She hadn't the faintest. Never even having allowed herself to get carried away by flights of fancy and false optimism —not like Rico, who had a knack for looking on the bright side.

And where had it gotten him?

Six feet under. Which was why she needed to perform this sad chore in the first place.

She sighed and tossed a stack of magazines in the garbage. On the top shelf of their closet behind where the magazines had been, she found an old photo album. Just the thing she needed. Maybe it would contain a few more humanizing touches for the small funeral service they'd be holding in a couple days' time.

The old leather cover was worn and patchy, but the photos inside were crisp and full of life. The five of them—Gloria and her four strapping brothers— sat on the retaining wall behind their small home, sticking out their tongues and making silly faces at the camera, little Pablo nothing more than an infant then. She remembered it well, could almost hear Mama shouting at them to behave and take a nice picture for once.

The next picture showed Rico and her father

wearing dirty trousers and work boots but no shirts, their bronzed skin made that much darker by hours in the hot afternoon sun. She remembered that day well, too. It was the day they had put that same retaining wall in the backyard to keep the little ones from stumbling up the hill and into the street behind.

Gloria turned the page, feeling grateful she had so many good memories with her brother given she'd never be able to form any new ones again.

A torn photograph fell into her lap, and she picked it up—a close-up of Rico's face, creased and torn clean down the middle, but still clearly showing his joyful smile and knowing eyes.

But what had he known really? Back then his life had been so full of potential. He hadn't yet signed up for the Air Force and he was still finding time to paint or sketch every day. They had been so happy then. Even Mama had been hale and healthy, an active part of the family still.

The saddest part of all? That the picture had been taken one short year ago.

Short in time, but long in memories—most of them grim. Gloria decided to hang on to this photo for herself. As she lovingly tucked it into her pocket-book, she couldn't help but wonder why this particular photo had been so carelessly maintained when other, much older pictures were still in pristine condition.

And what had happened to its other half?

Time passes. James's whiskers grow long and dirty, his bones become rigid and frail. He's hungry, tired, sore, scared. He has nothing to offer his captors, no vital information, no secret strategies—but still they keep him, hidden so well that apparently none of the search-and-rescue teams can find him.

He tries to remember Deborah's smile, the way her lips felt on his when they kissed under the night sky. But the memory feels artificial, like something he read about perhaps, only experienced vicariously rather than for himself.

Nothing feels real, save his one anchor to reality —to the hope of a life outside of this dank prison. The woman. The picture.

It is she, not Deborah, who comforts him in the night, who dances through his mind on a perpetual loop of invented memories. He imagines her life, what she must be doing every moment. Picking out the ripest tomatoes at the local grocer, reading a dime store novel while tucked away under the covers of her plush bed, taking a hike on a steep nature trail, stopping frequently to examine the tiny blooms along the road.

Her life is a pleasant, perfect event. Not like here. And if he manages to make it out with his life, he'll find her, thank her for saving him from madness, possibly even death. For it is his imaginings of her life that give him hope, the strength to take the abuse, the deprivation, and to survive his prison.

She is the reason he is still standing when they finally come to liberate him, the reason he can answer their questions with sure, confident answers rather than jagged sobs and hoarse whispers like the others they've saved from the encampment. She has meant the difference between life and death for him, but still he doesn't even know her name.

They fly him back to the States, admit him to a VA hospital. The doctor says he can't go home until he's regained some of his strength. The war is coming to a close now and soon his life can return to normal. But he doesn't know what exactly normal means anymore. His normal had become a cramped cell on foreign soil, the specter of death looming over him every second of every day. His guardian angel had delivered him from that fate, and now maybe she could save him from the horrifying prospect of *normal*. He doesn't want to return, only wants to move forward—to find the mysterious woman in the tattered photo he still clutches in his weakened grasp.

He must thank her, but first he has to figure out who she is and where he can find her.

Chapter 4

The hot air felt stagnant in the windowless factory. Gloria suppressed a cough, but still the dust continued to tickle her throat and burn her eyes. This was her life now, possibly forever. With Rico gone, she needed to work even harder both at home and on the assembly line to support her family.

Mama's medicine was expensive, but also non-negotiable. She couldn't imagine losing her dear mother so soon after her big brother. Meanwhile Papa was at work so often they rarely even saw him anymore. He didn't make near what he was worth, being an illegal worker.

She, having been born in the States like her younger siblings, could at least find somewhat more stable work. But she was still an unskilled, uneducated woman with brown skin and what some might call a bad attitude. She didn't find it at all fair that life had to be so difficult when her family worked so hard and were such good people. Still, she knew this job was the best she could get, and she was grateful for it.

Of course, now that she'd increased her hours, taking care of the household fell largely to her eldest living brother, Hector, who was only eleven. At that age boys should be outside climbing trees and riding bikes, not making lunch for their younger brothers or ensuring Mama took her medicine every four hours as instructed by the doctor.

Gloria's job involved quality control, inspecting the completed part to make sure there were no errors. Her part would be combined with other parts to form an engine, which would then go into a machine of some kind. What kind she still wasn't sure. Her mind often wandered as she ran her hands over the amalgamation of metal gears, springs, and rods.

She'd picture a better life for her family: Mama healthy again, dancing around the living room while Papa—who no longer had to work fourteen hours per day—held her close and crooned in her ear. Rico holding an art show downtown, selling his paintings for hundreds, even thousands of dollars, to wealthy socialites. She, at college, working toward a degree. In what, she didn't know. She only knew she wanted to learn about the many paths life had to offer before settling on the one that would best suit her.

Only... This life had a single path, one that involved working hard, making barely enough to scrape by until the day she died from sheer exhaustion. Perhaps she would marry, perhaps not. Why bring more children into such an impoverished, hopeless world?

Oh, she was happy for those few moments each day where she sat on the end of Mama's bed and allowed her to braid her long, dark hair before going to bed, when she told bedtime stories to her brothers, or listened to Papa's beautiful voice as he sang songs from the old country. Those moments were what kept her going for the long stretches in between when her muscles ached and her eyelids felt heavy.

A coworker came over and said hello, breaking her of her reverie.

"This is my last day, so I wanted to make sure I said good-bye," she announced, shooting a bright smile Gloria's way.

"Good-bye?" Gloria continued to examine her

part as the woman she hardly knew engaged her in conversation.

"Yes, I'm headed West. There's a new factory opening up in California, and it pays almost double what they give us here. Figured I might as well give it a shot, you know? Anyway, I guess this is it. Bye." She waved and headed toward the exit.

"Wait," Gloria called, imagining how different life could be for her family with a little extra financial padding. Papa could even stop working and stay home with the family. Yes, with a better job, Gloria could take care of them all, give each of them a better life. And who knew? Maybe the new factory wasn't quite so hot or dusty. Maybe her life could be better, too.

"Mind telling me a bit more about this new factory? Are they still looking to hire? Do you think...*I* could apply?"

The woman walked back her way and placed a business card in Gloria's hand. "Ask for Frank. And, hey, I hope to see you there. It would be nice to have a familiar face around."

Gloria stuffed the card into her pocket. Was this her golden ticket to a better life?

The opportunity loomed large in her mind. Yet still she hesitated. Her entire life had been in Texas.

Would this new job be so much better that it would be worth uprooting all of them? Taking Mama away from her doctor? What if things only got worse?

Part of her wanted so desperately to go, but another hidden part yearned to stay.

This wasn't a decision she could make herself. She'd leave it in God's hands. "Please," she whispered. "Father, show me a sign. Tell me the right path." Feeling relieved of the burden of this weighty decision, she returned her full focus to the assembly line. And she knew that, sooner or later, she'd receive a sign.

How she hoped it would be sooner.

The way James saw it, he'd spent all those months in the commies' prison; he didn't want to spend another day being held prisoner by anyone else. Even if the whitewashed walls of his current holding cell were that of a hospital room rather than a POW camp, he refused to be confined for another moment. He'd wasted too much time already.

"You need to rest up and regain some strength," the nurse said sweetly while changing his IV bag.

But James argued with the medical staff at every

turn. He so desperately needed to break free and find the woman whose picture he'd held close to his heart for what felt like forever.

Finally, they agreed to release James into the care of his buddy Tommy. It only took a bit of gentle prodding to get his old friend to make the long trip to sign him out of the hospital.

Tommy looked like a new man, one James almost didn't recognize when he stepped into the tiny hospital room and grabbed James's luggage.

"You look a little worse for wear there, Jimbo. Are you sure you want to head home? I saw that nurse you've got. What a looker." He let out a low, long whistle. "You sure it's not worth sticking around a little longer to try and make sweet with her?"

James didn't have the energy to laugh, but he did smile. "Nah, I'm ready to get home." He knew if he revealed his plan too soon, Tommy would turn around and bring him right back here—and James knew better than to let that happen.

"How you been, Tommy? Did you ever marry that girl of yours?"

Tommy spoke with a huge grin plastered on his lovesick face. "Sure did. And we're expecting. Should be any day now."

James stopped walking and gave his friend a long

hug, ending it with a few quick pats on his back. "I'm so happy for you, Tom. I can't believe you're going to be somebody's father. I mean, it seems like only yesterday we were—"

"Hey, not a word about that. Somehow Diana always manages to hear, even if there's half a world between us." He laughed and slapped James on the back as they walked through the parking lot. "It's so good to have you back."

But despite Tommy's words, James didn't feel as if he had returned.

He felt as if he was back at camp that first night with Tommy when he had discovered the photo, as if the past year or so hadn't happened at all. The time spent in the enemy's prison had occurred as one long uninterrupted chain of days spent staring at the picture, imagining her life, shutting out everything else around him, because to pay attention would be to invite pain.

Now here Tommy was, still the same chipper fellow he'd always been—just taller, stronger, and happier. He'd emerged from the war a hero, while James was meek and frail. What would his life be like now if he'd done his tour of service and returned home with Tommy? If he'd come back to the States with a wife waiting in the wings, a child on the way?

It all felt far too grown up.

Of course, James would never again be that patriotic nineteen-year-old, eager to defend his country, still not quite understanding the full ramifications of such a decision.

He was no longer the same idealistic youth Deborah Walker had fallen in love with. He was a man now, hardened by a war that almost broke him.

And Deborah...he'd promised to return to her—only now it didn't seem fair, not when he'd begun such an intense one-sided relationship with the woman in the photo.

He needed to broach the topic with Tommy. Now that his friend had signed him out of the hospital and driven half of the way home, he doubted he'd turn around and take him back. James just needed to do his best to not sound *too* crazy when he asked for his help.

Tommy apparently had a lot on his mind as well. While James continued to plan the big reveal in his head, his friend spoke up. "There's something I, um, need to tell you."

"What?"

The expression on Tommy's face turned sour. "About your girl, Deborah. Well, as far as we all knew you were dead. Jim, you had been missing for such a long time. None of us thought it was possible that you... When they called me to tell me you had been found, I just couldn't believe it. I couldn't stop hugging Diana and thanking God for delivering you safe and sound."

James sighed and held his arm out the window to let the wind rush through his fingers. "Safe, yes, but sound I'm not so sure."

Tommy took his eyes away from the road to study James. The car swerved, forcing him to return his focus to the highway. "Everything's going to be okay now. You're home, Jimmy. You made it! And you can stay with me and Diana as long as you need to, but there's something else we need to talk about first. I have to make sure you know before you get your hopes up to high."

"Okay, lay it on me." James brought his hand back inside the car and rested it on his lap.

"Well, when you went MIA, I went to her house to let her know what had happened. I mean, I figured she should know, right? And well, she seemed really torn up about it. Of course, she did. She was your girl. Then when they called last week, told me you'd be coming home, I tried so hard to find her again so she could be here waiting for you too. Only she was nowhere to be found. I tried so hard, Jimmy. Honestly, I did. Someone told me she got married and moved away, but I don't know for sure if that's true. I'm so sorry. I know you've already lost so much, but maybe you haven't lost her yet. We can still find her. I could help you look. Anything to help you get your life back."

James held up a hand to stop Tommy before he could go any deeper into his long-winded apology. His offer to help find Deborah had created the perfect segue into what he *really* wanted to discuss. "It's okay. I didn't expect her to wait so many years without any news. If she's truly moved on, well then, I'm happy for her. Besides, we only had that one night together, and then hundreds apart."

He reached into his pocket and pulled out the photo to show Tommy.

"You still have that?" His friend chuckled, seemingly relieved by James's reaction to the news of Deborah.

"And somehow I know it. I just know that this picture saved my life. It was the only thing that kept me sane all those months, those years, with the enemy. This woman is more real to me than any memory I have of Deborah—or anything else for that matter. I have to find her, Tommy." He licked his lips and focused his pleading gaze on his friend. "Will you help me?"

"Help you?" Tommy asked with a baffled look on his face. "I wouldn't even know where to begin searching for the woman in that picture. For all you know, she's married...or dead...or something. And what do you know? It can't be much more that that."

"I understand all that. I do. But I've gotta find her. I just have to."

Tommy's expression softened and he hit the steering wheel playfully with the palm of his hand. "Well then, dag nab it. Let's go find us a mystery woman. But, uhh, let's get you some rest first. Are you okay staying with me and Diana tonight? You can sleep on the couch. I'm sorry we don't have something more comfortable."

"The couch will be perfect." James laid a hand on Tommy's shoulder. "Thank you for everything. You have no idea how much this means to me."

CHAPTER 5

As Gloria headed home from the factory, she began her search for some kind of sign to tell her whether she should go after the new job in California or stay put right there in Texas. She walked at a more leisurely pace than normal to make sure she didn't miss anything, but God, it seemed, was in no hurry to tell her His decision.

She arrived home every bit as confused as ever.

"What's wrong, *Mija*?" Mama asked as she brushed out Gloria's hair and worked it into a long, tight braid.

Gloria sighed. She couldn't burden her mother with this. Not until she knew for sure what the best course of action was. "Just tired, Mama. How was your day?"

She listened as her mother talked about her brothers' many antics, about how she was feeling so much better these days—a statement Gloria knew for certain was a lie. "Still, I do look forward to the school year. Summer seems so long this year, no?"

Summer, fall—what difference did it make? All the days felt the same. No end in sight. No rest, no salvation. A part of her wished she could have died in his place. It wasn't fair that Rico's life should be cut short when he had so many dreams he still needed to fulfill, while Gloria remained without anything to inspire her.

"Mama?" she asked, her voice cracking. "What did you want to be when you were a little girl?"

"What kind of question is this?" She finished tying Gloria's braid and urged her to turn around on the bed so they could sit facing each other, both with their legs crossed Indian-style.

Gloria shrugged. "I was just thinking about Rico and how he wanted to be an artist."

Mama laughed. "Oh, that boy. He was great at so many things."

"I still miss him, Mama. Every single day."

"I know."

They sat without saying anything else for a few moments. Mama tapped the heel of the brush against her knee pounding out a gentle rhythm. When she had finished with her song, she said, "You know...now that I think about it, my dream was always to become a mama. You and your brothers, you are my dream." She tried to lean forward to hug Gloria, but the effort was too much.

Gloria happily stood and came to wrap her arms around her mother.

"Thank you, Mama," she whispered and then kissed the part in her mother's hair.

She let herself out of the room and went to make supper for her family. She still had no idea what to do about California, but talking to her mother had given her a great deal of relief. Her dream, too, was to be a part of a big, loving family—and, luckily, she already was.

The rest would come in time, if she was patient and trusted in both God and in herself to make the right decision.

James spent a couple days catching up with Tommy and Diana. They even paid him the honor of naming him the godfather for their unborn child—an honor he hadn't the slightest idea what to do with, but felt glad to have all the same. When the topics for conversation finally dwindled, James felt the time had come to remind his friend of the promise he'd made to aid in his search.

"About that..." Tommy ran his hands through his hair, which was a few too inches long according to military standards. "You see Diana, right? How close she is to popping? I can't just leave to go on a wild goose chase for some woman you're stuck on. I want to help you, I do, but I have to put my family first. You understand, right?"

None of this surprised James, but it still stung. He held his breath rather than sigh. "Can you drive me to base? I'll get myself home afterward."

Tommy's eyes searched his, but James refused to back down. Finally, Tommy sighed and stood. "If you're sure this is what you want. Just, please. Be careful, Jim. I already lost you once, and I can't—" His voice broke on that last word. "Little baby Morrison is going to need a godfather. And I'm going to need you too."

James laughed to lighten the mood. "C'mon, Tom. It's not like I'm flying back into a war zone. I'm just trying to find someone who's come to mean a great deal to me. Uncle Sam's taking good care of me, and I'd hate to impose on you any longer than I have to. Like you said, you've got a baby coming any day now. Look, I promise to eat right, get some sleep. But if I don't at least try to find her, I'll always wonder. I at least need to know I tried. Now stop acting so serious and get in the car."

Tommy hugged him. "Maybe I should try to find this girl first, warn her there's a tall drink of crazy headed her way." He laughed and slapped his buddy on the back. "C'mon, let's get gone before Diana wakes up and wonders where I've gotten to."

Now that he knew Tommy supported him at least in principle, James spent the drive to base telling him about all the scenarios he had imagined for meeting the mystery woman, all the various scenes he had pictured in his mind while in captivity.

"Do you love her?" Tommy asked as he shifted the car into park.

"That's the thing. I don't know what I feel exactly, and I don't think I will until I see her face to face, until I get to talk to her."

"I've gotta hand it to you, this is turning out to be one heck of an romantic adventure. I hope you find her, and I hope it's love at first sight. Call me later today, okay? Just so I know you're doing okay."

"I will." James said as he got out of the car, eager to officially begin his search. "Wish me luck."

"You've got it, Jimbo. See ya soon." Tommy stuck his arm out from the open window and waved, then reversed and headed home to his wife.

James watched the car turn out onto the main street, then gathered his wits about him and walked inside.

"How can I help you?" the administrator asked while sifting through a stack of papers on his desk.

James told the man who he was, where he'd stayed during his time in Korea, and how desperately he needed to find a friend he'd lost touch with after the war. And just in case, he slid the balance of his first pension check across the counter before the clerk could offer any protest. "I appreciate you doing this favor for me. Truly."

Half an hour later, James emerged from the admin offices with a list of names and numbers clutched in his hand. Now he needed a taxi home so he could make a few—hundred—calls. Who knew? Perhaps before the day was through, he'd have uncovered the identity of his mystery woman.

Chapter 6

Gloria took the day off from work. While she couldn't really afford the missed income, she also couldn't risk getting even more worn out by forcing herself to go in. After all, that could result in a full week of lost income and quite possibly put her job at risk. So she stayed home and took to cleaning the house from top to bottom, taking frequent breaks to rest and rehydrate.

Around noon the phone rang, which was odd because they rarely received calls—especially during the summer months when the boys weren't in school.

"Hello?" she asked, pressing the receiver close to her ear.

"Good afternoon. May I please speak to Ricardo Flores the Third?"

She gulped and took in a deep breath as she puzzled over how much to reveal to this stranger. What if he was some salesman trying to hock his wares? But then again what if he was one of Rico's friends from the service? Whatever the case, the man behind the voice seemed desperate for an answer.

"Hello, Miss? Is Ricardo available?"

She shook her head and studied the pattern on the kitchen's linoleum floor. "No, I'm sorry. Rico... He died overseas." She found it strange how little emotion her voice held despite the weight of the news she'd been forced to deliver. Would it still be this difficult to talk about Rico in past tense after a few more years had passed?

"Oh."

Pause.

"I'm very sorry to have bothered you."

Pause.

"And I'm sorry for your loss."

Gloria waited for the man to speak again, but instead the receiver clicked over and the call ended. Why had this man sounded so stricken even before hearing of Rico's death? And why had he called in the first place?

Well, it seemed like she would never know. She hoped whatever the man had wanted, it wasn't important.

James spun the rotary to eight, then let it spin back into place. Four. Spin. Nine. Spin. The dial of numbers had become a blur. Each number had seven digits plus an area code, and he'd called maybe a hundred, maybe two hundred that morning. Still he was no closer to finding his mystery woman.

He listened as the phone rang, the receiver clicked over, a man answered. "Hello?"

"Hi, is this Harry Smith?"

"Sure is. What can I do you for?"

Luckily James had had enough time to practice his pitch, so it at least felt a bit less strange as he delivered it. "I'm Airman James Morgan, served in Korea back in 1951, and I believe our paths may have crossed back then. Well, at the bunk, I found a picture of a woman. She has dark hair and brown eyes, appears to be about eighteen, although I'd reckon she's at least twenty now. I know this sounds crazy, but I'm trying to figure out who she is and how I can get ahold of her. You got anything for me?"

"My apologies, Sir, but can't say that I do. Good luck though."

James thanked the man and hung up. At least he could count on his fellow servicemen to be cordial regarding his strange request.

Still, this method was getting him nowhere. For all he knew he could have already spoken to the man who left the picture behind but just hadn't realized it. Or, the more likely scenario, he could have met his end, taking any hope of James's uncovering the woman's identity with him.

No, he couldn't think like that.

He would find her; he would. Things would be far easier if he could show people the picture. Surely then he could jog a memory, find a lead.

"You've given it your best shot," Tommy said that evening when James stopped over for dinner at Diana's invitation. "Can't you call it a day? Find a new woman to obsess over. One who can love you back. One who you know for sure exists."

Diana shushed Tommy and offered James a steaming bowl of peas. "I, for one, think it's all terribly romantic. Would you have done all this for me if I'd been missing when you came home?"

"Aww, Jimmy, now you're making me look bad in front of the wife." Tommy sniggered. "Give up and move on for me? For the sake of my marriage?"

Diana chuckled good-naturedly as well, but James shook his head vigorously.

"I can't give up, not until I know for sure. Seems like I'm starting all my sentences this way lately, but *I know it's crazy*. I think I survived that camp for a reason and that reason has to do with this woman. She saved me, gave me something to look forward to, gave me a reason to get out alive. What if she needs my help now? Every time I try to give it up, to let her go, something tugs me back in the direction of this photo. And I look at it and feel as if she's calling out to me, telling me to find her."

Tommy let out a long puff of air. "That sounds so..."

"Utterly romantic," Diana finished. "You'll find her, James. We know you will."

The conversation turned to the baby and all the preparations Diana was making for the nursery in the spare bedroom of their home.

James pulled the skin off his fried chicken and sank his teeth into the juicy meat beneath, chewing thoughtfully and marveling at Diana's vast love for the unborn child she hadn't even met yet. Of course, *he* understood it perfectly.

When it seemed dinner had come to its end, James had firmly decided upon his next step. "I'm leaving tomorrow," he announced.

"Oh? And where are you going?" Diana asked.

James pulled out the list of names, numbers, and addresses he now kept with him at all times. He flipped through the pages until he found his next destination. "California."

"Umm, can we ask why?" Tommy said, taking the papers from James and puzzling over them.

"Simple. To find her."

"And how do you intend to do that?"

"I'm going to show her picture around to the men at base. Surely, someone will recognize her, or at least the man who'd kept her picture with him."

"And you chose California because?"

"Because I've exhausted all my options around here, and California is next on the list."

"But, Jimbo, what if—?" He was cut short when his wife placed a hand on his arm and shook her head.

"Well, I think that's a fine idea," Diana supplied. "Tommy will give you a ride to the bus station. Just tell us when."

"Bright and early. First thing tomorrow." James smiled as he took the list back from Tommy. "I have a good feeling about this."

CHAPTER 7

Gloria cradled the telephone in her hands long after the caller had already closed their connection. Funny how such a simple, routine call that probably meant nothing to the man could change everything for her. When he'd asked to speak to Rico, it was as if the words wrapped around her heart and attempted to squelch its beating once and for all.

She was surprised it hadn't happened before now, actually. Rico had been well loved by the community. He had lots of friends and admirers of the murals he painted around town whenever he had a moment to spare, which wasn't as often as any of them would have liked.

Staying in Texas meant constant reminders of what she'd lost, what they'd all lost. And even though it was her home, home didn't have quite the same appeal it once did, not without the company of her closest friend.

California, though, would provide a fresh start.

They'd all still have each other, the family—and who knew? Maybe Mama's health would improve in the new, more stable climate. The fresh sea air would be good for them all.

She'd been waiting for God to send her a sign, and this seemed as good as any. She'd tell her folks soon enough. Papa would grumble and complain, but ultimately she knew he'd be grateful for the momentary break for his work. They'd find Mama a new doctor, the boys a new school. Everything would be okay, but first...

She returned to her bedroom and fished the tiny white card from her top dresser drawer, took a deep breath, and then dialed the number displayed on its surface.

"Why, yes. Yes, we are still hiring," a man named Frank answered. "Come on down for a quick interview, bring your references, and we'll see what we can do."

California was a long way to travel, and it would take every last penny the family could spare to get her there—but she'd made up her mind, and now there was no turning back.

James sucked the sweet sea breeze in through his nostrils. The air seemed fresher here, the world more open to possibilities. It invigorated him, helped him press on with his journey to find the woman in the photo.

But no one at the base had any good leads for him. One man thought he recognized the woman as Peggy, even gave James her address so he could meet her face to face. When he arrived at Peggy's apartment holding up a big bouquet of flowers, he wondered how the man had even seen the likeness between these two totally different looking women. Peggy was pretty, had the same full lips, but she was also a redhead, whereas his girl had dark, silky hair.

Still, a lead was a lead.

He showed Peggy the photo and talked with her about his search over tea.

"So you have no idea who she is, but you've been carrying her photo around all this time, hoping to find her?"

James nodded and eagerly accepted the picture when she handed it back to him. It always felt like a loss letting go of it, even if only for a second. "That's right." He tucked the photo safely back into his pocket. "I need to thank her for saving me life."

Peggy laughed good-naturedly. "She didn't save your life, James. You did that all on your own."

He shrugged. "Whatever the case may be, I have to find her, or I'll always wonder. I believe I found this picture for a reason, and I just can't rest until I find out what that reason is. I know it doesn't make a whole heck of a lot of sense, but I can feel it in my bones. I need to do this."

"Who cares much about sense these days? Most of us have too much sense for our own good anyway." Peggy batted her eyelashes and offered him the plate of lemon cookies again, but James declined.

"Well, if things don't turn out quite as expected, you know where to find me. I'd love to accompany you to dinner if you're ever back in town. Until then, good luck." She kissed him on the cheek and showed him out of the apartment.

Dinner, now there was an idea. The tea had been pleasant, but had really only stoked his appetite for something more substantial. He thought about knocking on Peggy's door again, inviting her to join him—she was, after all, a good looking and pleasant woman—but he also didn't want to give her any false hope.

His attentions belonged unequivocally to the woman in the picture, at least until further notice.

His stomach growled again, and he remembered passing by a pleasant looking diner on his ride over to see Peggy. He hopped a bus for the short ride back, his feet much too tired to carry him the full way.

As he rode toward his destination, he contemplated his journey. He'd started the search with his unit and the families of the airmen killed in the crash. After that, he'd moved onto one of the other B-29 squadrons that had operated over in Korea. He'd moved on to California, which also seemed to be a dead end.

So what next?

New Mexico might turn up a few good leads. Really, he just needed one—one perfect lead to find the woman he sought. As the bus approached his stop, he wondered why his search had thus far borne no fruit. The picture had come into his life for a reason, he was sure of that, so why had it been so difficult to find its subject? Wasn't *she* the reason for all this?

James refused to accept that fate had given him that photo as nothing more than a talisman. There had to be a greater significance. Didn't there?

Hungry. He was just hungry and tired, his body still weak from his imprisonment abroad. He was doing too much too soon, but at the same time it wasn't anywhere near enough.

A hot meal would do him a world of good. He slipped off the bus, planning to order the meatloaf.

And that's precisely when he saw her, alive, in the flesh, and standing right before him.

CHAPTER 8

"You want me to pay how much per month for this apartment?" Gloria asked again, her eyes squinting at the obscene number on the papers the building manager had handed her.

"Look, doll. That's just the way it is." He plucked at a suspender and frowned. "Don't you have a husband to take care of these sorts of things?"

Gloria did her best to remain pleasant, even though she'd had loved to give him a piece of her mind regarding what women could and could not do for themselves. "No, you're going to have to deal with me." She signed the lease and handed it back to him. "I'll take it. When can I move my things in?"

"The place is yours. Soon as you bring me a

check for the deposit." He gave her an avaricious grin.

"Oh, right. Do you have a Star bank around here?"

"Right around the corner, doll. But I can't promise I won't sell it to somebody else while you go. Everyone and their mother wants to live in *my* complex."

She sincerely doubted that, given the water stains in the hallway and the worn tread on the carpeting, but California was expensive; this place was all she could afford even when taking into account the salary of her better-paying job. "I'll do my best to hurry," she said as she turned to walk away.

The sting of the man's gaze bore into her thighs as she rushed out of his smoke-filled office. She exited the building, taking a quick glance back at the antiquated brownstone. The two-bedroom apartment the manager had shown her was only about half the size of their current ranch-style home in Texas. Of course, it meant all the boys would be jammed into a single room while Gloria would be resigned to the couch, but she hardly spent anytime in her room as it was, because when she wasn't working, the terrible loneliness of having a room all to herself was more than she could bear.

She needed a few minutes to herself to get her head on straight. Yes, God wanted her to come here, but following His plan hadn't always proven to be easy—especially not for Gloria. Maybe a quick trip to the pier she had spied when coming into town would help her breathe easy again, give her the strength she needed to sign for her family's new life right on the dotted line of the rental agreement.

She spotted a bus standing at its stop across the way and hurried across traffic to catch it. Luckily her legs were strong and toned from all those mornings walking to and from the factory.

A man slipped past her as she boarded the bus. Their arms brushed against one another, and gave her a static shock. The doors hissing shut behind her startled her briefly.

"Hope you're having a nice day," the driver said as she smiled and paid her fare.

The engine revved and the bus started up again. A flash of green caught Gloria's eye as they pulled away from the curb.

"Hey, hey, wait! Stop! Wait!" The same man who had just gotten off now shouted and pounded on the sealed door.

"Sorry," the driver said more to her than the man running after them. "I'm on a tight schedule here. Can't afford to be late."

But the man persisted. "Wait, Miss! I need to speak to you! Stop the bus! I..." His voice faded beneath the symphony of the city traffic.

Gloria took her seat and stared at him from the bus's rear window. Why did she have the sneaking suspicion he had been trying to talk to her? What could that stranger possibly have had to say? She checked her belongings to make sure she hadn't dropped anything before brushing her concerns aside. No need to puff herself up with hot air. The man had clearly been after the driver or another patron of the bus, not her.

This was a whole new world. And even though she was all alone now, she'd soon build a fresh life upon the ashes of the one she'd willingly left behind.

The full lips, the dark walnut eyes so full of mystery, yet so inviting—it was definitely her. Her! James didn't get a proper look at her until after the doors had closed and the bus had started to pull away.

"Stop! Wait!" he cried, but it was no use. The driver refused to open the doors, and James was too short of breath to continue to chase the vehicle as it picked up speed and disappeared into the busy city streets.

James cursed under his breath, staring at the bus as it turned a corner and left his line of vision. He stood there for a while as busy pedestrians passed him on both sides.

It had been her, no doubt about it. She was real, and she was here in California. Hope swelled in his chest. If he had found her once, he could find her again. He *would* find her again.

He turned to walk back toward the diner, which sat just across the street from the bus stop. The smile didn't leave his face the whole way.

She was real. She was here. And sooner or later they would bump into each other again. He would finally get the chance to speak with her, to learn her name, to thank her for all she'd done for him, even though she didn't have the slightest clue she'd done a thing, let alone so much.

At the diner, he ordered the meatloaf and a tall glass of Coke. He took a seat facing the large window that looked out onto the street and stayed until closing time. The next day he came back bright and early and took up his station again. He came the day after that too—and the day after that.

On the fifth day, one of the waitresses came by to chat with him as she topped off his cup of Joe. "You know the girls are starting to tell stories about you?"

James reluctantly tore his vision away from the window and looked up at the pretty blonde with bright red lipstick.

She smiled at him and took a seat on the opposite side of the booth. "Pam thinks you're an undercover cop on a stakeout, but I said, 'Pam, that's ridiculous. He doesn't look a thing like a cop.' Then there's Rosemary. She thinks you've got a case of that —what do they call it?—*amnesia*, and that you keep coming in here to try to jog your memory because you can't remember where your home is and so you don't really have anywhere else to go." She leaned forward conspiratorially. "But me? I think you're waiting for somebody who means an awful lot to you."

"Oh?" James raised an eyebrow and took a sip of the piping hot coffee.

"I'm right, aren't I? I knew it," she squealed. "Name's Betty Jo by the way."

He took the hand she reached across the table in greeting.

"And who might you be?"

"James," he said, purposefully avoiding his military title so as not to create an even bigger fuss.

"How do you do, James? Now, tell me, because I'm dying to know. Is my little theory correct?"

He nodded and her smile grew even wider.

"I knew it! Who is she?"

He took her photo out of his breast pocket and pushed it across the table to Betty Jo.

Her mouth formed an O as she studied the picture, then looked back up at him with excitement brimming in her eyes. "Wow, she's a real beauty, James. That's some girl you've got there. What's her name?"

James sighed. "That's the thing, I don't know."

An expression of concern flashed across her face, but she quickly rearranged her features back into a smile. "So Rosemary's right too? About the amnesia?"

He chuckled. "No, no. No amnesia here." And he launched into his story about finding the picture, being taken prisoner, and returning home to start his search.

The whole time Betty Jo listened with her chin resting on her palm, completely enraptured. When he'd finished, she said, "Well, James, I sure hope you find her. And that, when you do, she knows how lucky she is to have caught your eye. If it helps, I'll keep an eye out for her too. We'll find her for you, James."

"Thank you, Miss. Thank you."

"Oh, it's nothing. The girls and I are happy to help. But maybe you should go and get some rest, huh? It can't be easy sitting in that stiff little booth from sun up to sun down, day in and day out. I'll cover this shift. Go and grab some shut-eye, okay?"

"You're right. I am pretty sore." He stood and stretched. "Here's my number at the hotel. Call me if anything comes up, okay?"

"I will. You better believe it. Good night, honey. Get some sleep."

Settled back into his hotel room, he decided to place a quick call to check in with Tommy back home.

Tommy answered on the first ring. "James! Where have you been? I've been going crazy trying to get ahold of you! Diana's had her baby, a boy! We named him after you, James, after his godfather. You've gotta get back here and see him. We leave the hospital day after tomorrow. Diana's been asking after you, too. Oh, you should see him, Jimbo. You should see my little boy."

"Congratulations," James said when at last Tommy paused to take a quick breath. "I'm so happy for you and Diana. I'll be on the first flight home, but first there's something I have to do real quick."

CHAPTER 9

Gloria flipped through her brother's notebook, pausing occasionally to lightly run her fingers over the lifelike images. Rico's art always brought her back to a happier time, especially now as she reminisced about walking home from school with Rico each weekday afternoon.

When he was in fifth grade and she in third, Rico had started to come into his own as an artist. He'd draw the cartoons made popular by the cinema and exchange them with his classmates for gumballs, candy buttons, and other sweets Mama never allowed them at home. Most days he'd have a treat saved for her, even though she knew it must have been nothing short of torture to keep the precious candy stowed away in his desk all day.

He'd always been a good brother, and she'd done her best to return the favor whenever she could. Like the time Rico accidentally shattered Mama's favorite vase while roughhousing with his neighborhood friends. He was already on a short leash with Papa for earning a poor grade on his latest Geography test, so Gloria herself had tearfully confessed to the crime.

Today, she finished packing up Papa's things and moved on to those of her younger brothers, also filled with many memories. From hand-me-downs to family pictures and tattered school notebooks, Rico lived not just within every nook and cranny of that house but also every single object inside of it.

She would never be free of him—not that she wanted to forget her brother, only the pain that came with missing him. Still, she could leave Texas, move halfway across the world, even, and Rico would remain by her side every single step of the way.

Boxing up all her memories only to unpack them in her future home proved that she'd always miss him, no matter how much time or distance passed between her old life and the new one she was building now.

"Mama," she called shrugging into a light sweater. "I'm just going out for a bit. I'll come home and finish up soon."

She rushed out before her mother could see the

tears pooling at the corners of her eyes. Luckily, the neighbors allowed them to borrow their station wagon for doctor's visits and emergencies as long as they filled the tank up before returning it. This definitely qualified as an emergency in her mind. She just hoped nothing urgent happened while she was away, but she had to do this one thing before she could fully pack up her old life, had to do it for herself.

Gravel crunched under the tires of the station wagon as Gloria pulled into the cemetery. Large, aged trees stood guard, separating the final resting places of the interred soldiers from the busy road beyond. The clouds hung low over the rolling hills as if they too had come to say good-bye.

Gloria walked reverently toward the northernmost corner of the lot, mentally preparing for the newest installment in this seemingly never-ending series of goodbyes. But this time she was really leaving him behind—at least it felt that way. She knew they'd all think of him often, but no one in the family would be able to physically visit his grave and it would be all her fault for moving them away from here.

What choice did she have, though? Sure, the new apartment would be smaller, but the higher salary meant Papa wouldn't have to work so hard anymore, that he could enjoy Mama's final days with her, that her brother Hector wouldn't have to take over as the primary caregiver, effectively ending his childhood before he reached the age of twelve. Her path was clear, and it led to California.

She knelt down, letting her bare knees sink into the spongy grass. Now she just had to find the words to say all that was in her heart.

James hated to leave California when he was so close to locating his mystery woman, but he also wanted to be there for his friend and to meet his new godson. A few days' absence wouldn't harm him any, especially not when Betty Jo and the other women at the diner had so eagerly agreed to be on the lookout for him.

He managed some sleep on the plane ride back to Texas, but still he was exhausted as he drove toward the VA hospital in a borrowed car. James knew he needed to establish an official home base now that he was back in the States to stay, but all that would come in good time.

Today he would meet his godson, and some day

soon he would meet his girl. Now that he'd seen her up close, he knew beyond a shadow of a doubt that the feeling he had for her was none other than love —love at its finest.

A few short years ago he hadn't believed in love at all. Now he not only believed twice over, but he also believed in love at first sight. How had he turned out to be such a hopeless romantic?

The war, no doubt, had changed him. Now that he'd lost freedom, love, happiness, he knew how much they were to be cherished, clung to at any opportunity they presented themselves.

When he found his woman—and for now he did think of her as his—he would tell her every single day how beautiful he found her, how much he appreciated her very existence. That is, provided she agreed to give him the time of day.

But how could she refuse him when their love story was already written? Before they'd even met anywhere outside his dreams?

He hoped all the women he'd spoken with on his journey—Diana, Peggy, Betty Jo—were right, and that she would find this all blissfully romantic and not frightening.

Soon he would have his answers, know her heart,

her name—but first he needed to meet another very special individual.

Tommy, Diana, and their new son, little James, were expecting him that morning. He'd already stopped off at the store to find flowers for Diana, a blanket for the baby, and a congratulatory cigar for his friend.

Would he, too, soon know the joy that came with fatherhood? It was such an exciting thought, his whole life coming together—and in the very near future.

The VA complex came into view as he turned onto the busy lane. He passed the admin building where he'd obtained the list of contacts that had proved essential to his search.

On the left, there was a veterans' cemetery where many of his fellow servicemen had been buried. Although the day was bright, a low fog clung to the earth, giving the place an ethereal glow. He continued to study the graveyard as he drove, to offer prayers for those who had fallen in the name of freedom.

And then he saw a dark-haired woman crouched near one of the fresher interments. He couldn't make out much more than her silhouette, but something told him he needed to stop.

He parked on a hill and walked down.

She didn't notice him at first as she sobbed.

He didn't mean to eaves drop, but he also hated to interrupt as she told the deceased of all the things she wished she'd been brave enough to say when he'd been alive —so instead he stood there, unmoving, but full of feeling.

And when she at last came to realize his presence, she turned to face him, splotches of red covering her tear-stained cheeks. But even the puffy eyes, the reddened skin, the windblown hair did nothing to hamper her beauty.

It was *her*. Again. This time he'd found her right here in his hometown.

Now he just needed to find the right words to tell her everything she'd come to mean to him. James took a deep breath and braced himself for what he was sure would become the first moment of the rest of his life.

Chapter 10

She noticed his shadow first, the way it grew darker as it approached, how his shoulder aligned perfectly with the dates carved into Rico's tombstone. She assumed he had come to pay his respects to some other fallen solider, but his shadow remained cast across Rico's grave like some sort of dark angel.

As if talking to the lifeless headstone hadn't been difficult enough, she certainly couldn't do so with an audience. She rose to her feet slowly, turned toward the stranger. "Hello, there. Were you a friend of Ricardo's?"

He opened his mouth but didn't speak. His eyes glistened with the beginnings of tears, though his expression seemed one of joy rather than grief.

"Did you know my brother?" she repeated. "Did you know Rico?"

He still didn't speak, and for a moment she wondered whether he understood English. She turned her back to him and looked toward Rico's headstone once more. She still had so much she needed to say.

Maybe she could take a quick drive around the block, come back after the stranger had done whatever he came here to do, grab a few more minutes of privacy with her brother, say a proper good-bye.

"Look." She sighed. "He's all yours. I'm going." She pushed her purse strap higher up her shoulder and brushed past the stranger, careful not to walk on any of the fresh graves. No matter how hasty her departure, she still needed to show proper respect for the dead.

"W-wait!" the man called, his voice panicked... and somehow familiar. He jogged to catch up with her. When he reached her side, he groped about in his pocket and extended her a small paper with a tear down one side.

She studied him cautiously, ultimately deciding that *strange* didn't necessarily equate to *dangerous*. He pushed the paper toward her again, and she took it into her own hands.

It wasn't a paper, but a photo—one she recognized instantly as the missing half of the picture from Rico's album. "This... this is me. How did you get it?"

"Let me buy you a Coke," he said. "I'll explain everything."

Gloria didn't have to think twice about his offer. She was eager to grab any bits of information about her brother's last days she could get. Clearly, from the way his eyes swelled with tears and a smile played at the corners of his mouth, this man had one fantastic story to tell.

And she wanted to make sure she heard every last word.

It took James longer than he would have liked to find his words. But he couldn't stop staring at the living version of the dream he'd carried with him for so long. She was so much like he'd imagined her, yet so uniquely real at the same time. Her eyes were brighter in life than they had appeared in the photo. She was taller than he'd envisioned her too, more shapely with a fuller chest and hips. And she moved gracefully as he'd known she would.

She studied him for a moment but then agreed. "I'll be driving myself though. Hope that's all right with you."

"Yes, yes, of course," James answered, his voice came out strong as if any words he had uttered previously in his life were just practice for these, the first in the most important conversation. He walked her over to the station wagon and opened the door for her as his father had taught him to do for a lady.

"Before you go, please." He said as she sank into the car's seat. "Tell me your name."

She stuck the key in the ignition. "It's Gloria. I am—well, was—Rico's sister."

"Gloria." He liked how the word required him to

pucker his lips to get the roundness of the O. "I'm James."

She smiled as she latched the buckle on her seatbelt. "Nice to meet you, James. Should we head over to the All American?"

"Sure thing. I'll follow you there." He jogged to his own borrowed vehicle and started up the engine. It was a short drive to the All American diner, and for that he was thankful. A part of him worried she'd disappear again before he could tell her his story, but she turned into the crowded parking lot as promised and got out of her car before he could offer to open the door for her.

Inside, he ordered them both Cokes and a plate of onion rings to share. He took out the picture again and handed it her way. "I believe this is yours."

"Well, it was Rico's actually. I have the other half of it at home." She laughed wistfully. "I had no idea he'd taken it overseas. Were you with him when he...?" She let the question linger.

"No, I'm sorry. I didn't have the chance to meet him, although he sounds like a swell guy. I mean, to have a sister like you."

A confused expression crossed her face, and she bit her lower lip. "I don't understand. How did you get this picture then? How did you find me?"

The waitress arrived and placed their Cokes in front of them.

James waited for her to return to the kitchen before continuing. "That's why I wanted to talk to you."

"I'm listening." She stirred her soda with her straw and took a sip.

"Gloria, I know you don't know me, but you saved my life. I will forever be thankful to you—and to Rico—for that."

Her smiled turned to a frown as she crossed her arms defensively across her chest and leaned back in the booth. "I—I don't understand. How could I have...?"

Luckily, he had rehearsed this speech in his head many times and knew exactly how he wanted to deliver it now.

Gloria listened silently, warming to him as he continued. She even reached across the table to rub his hand in sympathy when he described the crash of the Saving Grace, being taken into the POW camp.

He stopped at the part where he came home, having resolved to find and thank her.

"Wow," she whispered when he had finished. "That's some story. And you did it too. You actually did it. You found me even though you had so little to go on."

"That picture of you, it saved my life, Gloria. I will always be so grateful to both you and your brother for leaving it there for me to find."

"You really think it saved your life?" She asked, something like hope in her eyes.

"I know it did..." He reached across the table and grabbed both of her hands in his own. "Gloria—" He couldn't get past how great her name felt on his lips. "Do you believe that things happen for a reason?"

Her eyes searched his. "Like signs from God telling you where to go?"

"Exactly."

"Yes, I do, James. Very much."

"Your picture was a sign, one I couldn't ignore. I've waited for this moment for so long, and now that it's here I don't want it to end. Let me buy you dinner, so we can talk longer."

She squeezed his hands, and a pulsing energy shot through him. "I'd like that," came her reply.

CHAPTER 11

Gloria surprised herself by agreeing to stay for

dinner. She had so much packing to do in preparation for the family's move to California, and she still had things she needed to say to Rico, too. But something about James compelled her to stay and listen.

It wasn't just that he, too, believed in God's signs or that he had followed them all the way to her. There was a kindness, a gentleness about him that she didn't often sense in others, especially men.

Speaking with James made her feel oddly connected to Rico, as if by keeping her picture safe all these years had given him a special bond to her brother.

"First I tried calling at least a couple hundred folks," he explained between bites of his hot turkey sandwich and mashed potatoes.

"Wait a sec." Gloria took a sip of Coke—her third of the evening—to wet her throat. "You called?"

"Yes, a whole bunch of folks from the list. That didn't get me anywhere though, so I—"

"James, I *remember* that call. Now I know why your voice sounds so familiar. You talked to me that day!"

"I did?" He smiled and pushed another forkful of mashed potatoes into his mouth.

"You did. I can't believe it. If I'd only known, I

could have saved you all this trouble in searching for me."

James chuckled. "That's not the only time our paths nearly crossed. I saw you get on a bus in California. I tried to get your attention, but I couldn't keep up."

"That was *you*?" Gloria's jaw dropped in surprise, and she was grateful she'd already finished her meal for the evening.

"That was me." He winked, and a tingle flew down Gloria's spine and came to rest near her stomach. Oh, he was handsome with his strong jaw and high cheekbones. Why hadn't she noticed earlier?

Heat rose to her cheeks as he continued to smile. "So you followed me to Texas from there?"

"No. I waited right by that bus stop for days hoping you'd come back. I came home to Texas to meet my new godson." He took another bite, helping her to relax back into the natural flow of conversation.

"Home?" she asked, admiring his strong hands as they maneuvered the utensils.

"Yes, home. What brings *you* to Texas?"

She shook her head, unable to believe all their near encounters. God had certainly intended to bring them together, but why did he have to be such a tease about it? "This is my home, too. I live a couple towns over. Rico is buried in that cemetery, and I was saying goodbye before..." She caught herself and stopped.

James offered her a reassuring smile. His eyes, however, betrayed his worry. "Gloria, what is it?"

She gulped. Why was this so hard to admit when only hours before she'd been absolutely certain going to California was the right decision?

James stayed quiet, waiting for her answer.

"Before I... leave. James, I'm moving to California in a few days."

She watched as the realization swept over him. "That's why you were...?"

"Yes, and if things were different, I'd love to spend more time getting to know you. But I have a lot of responsibilities. My mother, she's sick, and my father doesn't earn well because..." She stopped herself before revealing her parents' secret. No matter how much she wanted to trust James, she refused to put her parents in danger. "Then there's my three younger brothers to take care of, and all on such little money. California could be a better life for us. We're leaving in three days."

James nodded. "I understand, and I won't ask for anything more than you can give. Please, though, can we just have tonight? I've waited so long to meet you."

Gloria looked at the clock on the diner's wall. She felt guilty about how long she had already been gone. Mama had no idea where she'd gotten off to, and what if they needed the car for an emergency? Still, she so rarely did things for herself these days, and that would be especially true once they went to California and Gloria was forced to leave her few remaining friends behind. Besides, it seemed to mean so much to James—and she really did like him. Things would have been different if...

No, she chastised herself. Stop thinking about what comes later. Just enjoy now.

She took a deep breath and smiled. "I can do that."

James was glad she had agreed to stay, because he wasn't ready to let go of her just yet. They talked, ate dessert, and drank more Coke. It all felt so...natural. That was the only word for it really. And the more she told him about her life, the more he told her about his, the harder he fell for her.

Gloria was the one. He knew it now. So when the

diner closed for the night, he asked if she wouldn't mind sitting outside with him so they could keep talking. And he was overjoyed when she accepted.

"So you really made your little brothers think they had magical powers?" he asked as they sank down onto the cement curb to continue their chat.

"Yes, but only when they sleepwalked. Each night I'd sneak into their room and move things around, make special items appear that weren't there the night before. And they believed it for, oh, a good couple months before they caught on."

They both laughed. She hugged her knees to her chest and stared longingly into the night sky. The stars were out in full effect, providing a gorgeous backdrop to their evening.

James watched her as she smiled and launched into a new story about how she'd once tried to count all the stars in the heavens, but had stopped somewhere around two hundred, realizing there were far too many to ever accurately count.

"Gloria?"

"Yes?" She smiled at him, her teeth bright against the dark.

"I'd like to kiss you now. Would that be all right?"

She blushed, but nodded.

James leaned toward her slowly. He'd pictured

this moment so many times and wanted to make sure that he got it just right. He pressed his lips first to her rosy cheek and then to her full, beautiful lips. When he pulled away, she had tears in her eyes.

"What? What happened?" he pleaded, pulling her into his side so her head could rest on his shoulder.

"I just like you so much." The words cut straight to his heart. They implied a *but*, and he hated that. Things were supposed to be easy now that they were finally together, now that he knew his feelings for her amounted to love and was quite convinced she felt the same way, too.

When she didn't continue, he gave her a gently nudge. "So why is that a bad thing?"

"I'm leaving, James. This has to be the end, even though it's only just the beginning."

James thought back to the night he'd spent with his first love Deborah all those years ago. That, too, had ended the same night it began. He'd shipped off to Korea the next day, found Gloria's picture, been captured by the enemy, changed the course of his entire life.

Although he was now happy for his and Deborah's end and the chance it gave him to find Gloria, he also refused to let poor timing take love from him once more.

"*Stay*," he said firmly, having made up his mind.

She pulled herself out of his arms and looked into his eyes. "I can't. I have to take care of my family, and that means moving to California."

"Not if you marry me instead. Let me take care of them, too. Let me take care of *you*. I have a good pension and benefits. I could make a good life for you, Gloria. You are the reason I survived that camp, don't you see? You're the reason I'm still here. Let me devote the rest of my life to thanking you in whatever way I can."

She looked at it him as if he were crazy, but also as if she were suppressing a smile. "James, you can't be serious. We've only just met."

Now was his moment. He needed to get this exactly right. Nothing he ever said again would be anywhere near as important as this. He took a deep breath. "So what? Right is right. Did you know I fell in love with you long before we even met? Being with you now just confirms everything my heart already knew to be true. *I love you*, Gloria, and I want us to be together."

James took her back into his arms, felt her heart beating wildly against his chest. The craziest part of his proposal was that it didn't feel crazy at all. Being with Gloria felt right. It felt logical. It felt intended by something much larger than either of them alone.

Now she just needed to say yes, so they could begin their life together—their wonderful, beautiful, *destined* life together.

CHAPTER 12

Gloria wasn't sure she'd heard James correctly—not until he repeated his proposal. The scariest part? How easily she found herself tempted to say yes.

Love was not something she'd pictured for herself, not when so many responsibilities weighed on her shoulders already. But love held a very important place in her life already. Love was what kept her going even when she wanted to stay tucked in bed all day, to sleep her cares away. The most important thing in the world to her was her family—and wasn't that love?

James said he loved her now, and she believed him without hesitation. The sincerity in his eyes was impossible to ignore. But what would her family think? Would Mama be relieved to see her daughter married off before the sickness claimed her? Gloria didn't want to be *married off*, though. Her family still needed her. They could never survive without her. Papa didn't earn enough, and Hector was too young for such a major responsibility.

But James said he'd take care of them, too—and it seemed like he meant it. This whole evening seemed too good to be true, like the fulfillment of a dream she never knew she possessed. And now that it was laid out before her she wanted nothing more than to see it to reality.

Still, Rico had been the optimist of the family, and look where that had gotten him. Was it foolish to agree to James's offer? Could it be foolish not to? She still had so much to consider.

She looked up at him. The love in his eyes was unmistakable. It made her feel so warm, so protected, her life suddenly looked full of possibilities. All because of some chance encounter, all because this man—a good man—loved her.

She needed to say something, but she knew either a *yes* or a *no* would mean no going back, and she still needed time to speak to Mama and Papa, and to pray for direction.

"James..." she started.

He perked up, his posture now military straight as he waited for her response.

"I will..."

His eyes sparkled brighter than the stars. Oh, how she hated to let him down, but doubt had already killed so much of her happiness before. If she and James were to truly move forward together, she needed to clear it all away so they could have a sunny future together.

"Need some time to consider your offer."

He stood and lent her his hand to pull her up. "I understand. Can we meet again tomorrow? I'll wait here at the diner for you."

"Yes." She gave him a hug goodbye, although what she really wanted to do was kiss him. She also didn't want to give him false hope in case she had to say *no* when tomorrow came.

Oh, how she hoped this path was the right one for her, because she desperately wanted to run forward with James and to never look back.

§♠

James drove back to the Morrison's home after his whirlwind evening with Gloria. He hoped Tommy would understand, and he hoped he wouldn't wake the baby with his late arrival. But when he got there, Diana was up anyway feeding Little James his midnight meal.

"Jim," she said as he walked through the doorway and into their living room. "We'd wondered what happened to you." And then she saw the giant smile that hadn't left his face all evening.

"You found her, didn't you?"

He sat down beside her and wrapped an arm around her shoulder. "I did. Oh, Diana, I did."

"Tell me everything. I have all the time in the world. But first, there's someone who would like to say hello." She placed the baby in his arms, and his heart swelled even more than it already had.

This could be his future, too. Gloria only needed to say *yes* to unlock all the wonderful possibilities.

𓃑

He returned to the diner at opening, having only secured an hour or two of sleep, if that. He'd taken care of his godson and sent Diana to get some sleep. The baby provided great company as he paced through the house and thought about his beautiful evening with the woman he loved, the woman he hoped would soon be his wife.

He started just with coffee. An hour later, he ordered a plate of eggs sunny side up. Two hours after, he added a glass of water, then a hamburger and fries. Around three o'clock, he began to worry, so he had a strawberry milkshake to calm his nerves. When evening rolled around and Gloria still hadn't shown up, he was absolutely beside himself.

"What's wrong, honey?" a young and vibrant waitress brought him a fresh glass of water. "I just started my shift, but the other girls tell me you've been sitting here all day with that forlorn look on your face."

"I'm just waiting for someone, but I'm not sure if I missed her."

She nodded. "You wouldn't be waiting for that woman you sat here with all last night, would you? For Gloria?"

James's ears perked up at the mention of Gloria's name, a new spring of hope welling inside him. "Do you know her?"

"Sure do. We went to school together. She was on the quiet side, but nice."

This gave James an idea. "You wouldn't happen to know where she lives, would you?"

"Actually, I do." She wrote down an address on her order pad and tore it off for him.

James made sure to leave a very big tip before he darted out of the restaurant.

᠀

He found her home easily enough, but when he arrived, he was shocked to find that it was empty. All traces of furniture and personal belongings were absent. He saw only an endless stretch of freshly groomed carpet when he peered inside the large porch window.

But she'd said she was leaving in a few days, hadn't she? Had his proposal scared her away, made her decide to leave earlier than originally planned?

Of course it had. How stupid he had been to come on so strong. He'd had years to fall in love with her, to learn every contour of her face, but she'd known him for hardly twenty-four hours now, and for only six when he made his proposal.

He should have been more considerate, less forward. How could he have made such a colossal mistake?

But then he realized it wasn't himself he was angry with, but rather God. Why would he send so many signs leading James straight to Gloria only to offer him heartbreak in the end? Hadn't he suffered enough at the hands of the commies as they kept him confined to their dank prison for so many months on end?

He was a good person, darn it. He didn't deserve this, and Gloria didn't either. Even though she had decided to run away from the possibility of their life together, he knew the decision couldn't have come easily. He knew she cared for him, too. He could see it in her eyes, in every single gesture she made when they'd been together.

He sank down to the porch stoop, unable to leave. Leaving felt too final. Leaving meant he'd have to move on, find something new to do with his life, now that its sole purpose had been taken clean away from him.

He ran over all his options in his head, but his thoughts kept returning to Gloria. He took out the picture from his breast pocket and ran his thumb over her faded cheek. He sat there for a long time. The lack of sleep from the night before caught up with him, and he drifted off there on that unfamiliar stoop with his knees tucked into his chest and his head resting on his arms.

He awoke to a gentle nudge on his arms. When he looked up, she was there. He closed his eyes again, certain it was a dream.

But then she spoke. "James? James, are you all right?"

He darted to his feet, wiped the sleep from his eyes. "Gloria," was all he could manage to say.

She sat down beside him. The heat from her body warmed him up. "I came looking for you at the diner, but they told me you were here."

He still couldn't be sure this wasn't a dream. "But I thought..."

"That I was gone?" She laughed softly. "No, I came as soon as I could. We had to be out of the house for the new tenants today, which meant moving our things out and staying with family close by. And, well, because of all that, I had so much work to do before I could come to see you. But it did give me a lot of time to think about...about your offer."

"And?" James stood. Somehow he knew he couldn't take the news—whatever it may be—sitting down. He felt he needed to be standing the moment his life changed forever, standing and ready to move forward. Or to move on.

She reached for his hands and pulled herself up, clutching his hands in hers as if letting go wasn't an option. Her eyes searched his, and he knew. Before the words even escaped her mouth, he knew.

"And I'd like to accept. James, I'd like to be your wife, if you'll still have me."

Gloria powdered her nose and stared at herself in the vanity's mirror. She marveled at how flawless her skin looked, how perfect the ringlets in her hair hung beneath her veil. Yes, everything about this day was perfect—as was quickly becoming the story of her life.

It had all happened so quickly, really. First James's impassioned proposal, then telling her parents, buying a new home together in the suburbs. She'd insisted upon a small civil service, feeling no need to throw money away in exchange for a party that only lasted a single day. But the upcoming nuptials had given Mama a purpose despite her illness. Gloria marveled at all she had accomplished while sitting on the sofa and dialing various florists, cooks, and wedding guests on the phone.

And now the day had come. Mama proudly helped Gloria into the same vintage dress she had worn when she married Papa more than twenty years ago in Mexico. It had been the one thing she insisted upon bringing to America, should she ever have a daughter and the ability to pass it down. Less than a year later, Gloria had been born, but Mama never mentioned the dress until recently.

"Do you know why we named you Gloria?" she asked now as she applied rouge to her daughter's cheeks.

"For *Abuela*?" Gloria puckered her lips, so her mother could apply a berry-colored stain to her lips.

"It's more than that. Here, press." She extended a tissue toward Gloria, so she could set her lipstick into place. "I always knew you were a strong one like your *abuela*. I always knew you would bring greatness to our family. I just never knew how exactly until now. Gloria, you have changed everything for us. Do you know that?"

She hugged her mother tight. "Don't be silly."

"I'm very serious, *Mija*. Because of you we still have a home, and now Papa and I are even becoming citizens. After so many years of calling this country home, we finally can say we are Americans. That's all I wanted before I died, that I see my daughter happy, my sons taken care of, and that I become an American."

"I wish Rico were here." Gloria did her best not to cry and ruin her mascara.

"He is here, Gloria. Can't you feel him close by?"

Gloria smiled.

"Come now, your groom, he is waiting. Are you ready?"

Her father was waiting near the back door, and as Gloria and Mama arrived, he took her by the arm and walked her through the backyard toward the place where James stood waiting. He looked so handsome in his dress uniform.

Festive decorations lined their white picket fence. Friends and relatives sat huddled around the altar in folding chairs adored with ribbon. It was quite the scene, but Gloria couldn't appreciate it because she couldn't take her eyes off her groom as she walked toward him. Toward their beautiful future together.

Life was meant to be lived, not simply survived. She understood that now, and—oh—how she looked forward to every wonderful day that was yet to come.

ALL I HAVE TO DO IS DREAM

James loved the way Gloria looked when full with child—the sway of her hips as she scuttled around carrying the extra burden, the way her face and breasts filled out just a little extra, and her hair became thick and wavy. He never grew tired of it, just as he never grew tired of spoiling her and their four precious little girls. She had wanted to stop at Constance, but he had convinced her to try one final time for a son. He knew she craved a little boy every bit as much as he did, and besides, pregnancy suited her well.

When he returned home from work that evening and wrapped her in his arms, she saddled him with a kiss so ferocious, so needy, that he doubted they'd even stop at five. One day they'd have a whole brood of children running circles around the both of them —too in love with each other and with their family to have the heart to stop.

"Daddy! Daddy!" Beverly cried, racing into his arms and peppering his cheeks with kisses.

"Daddy!" Victoria said, tugging at the hem of his coat. "Look what I made in school." She held up a colorful finger painting for his appraisal.

"Da-da!" Even Constance, who was just learning to speak, seemed pleased by his arrival.

"There's *mi hijo*," his mother-in-law called from the couch where she sat with her swollen ankles propped up. "*Abuelo* and I have a special surprise for you after supper."

"What is it? What is it?" His little girls chanted, jumping up and down with excitement.

"Let's have supper first. Your mama has worked so hard to prepare it, after all. *Then*." Her eyes twinkled with mischief. "Then we will have your surprise."

The girls raced through dinner. Even James found himself shoveling in each spoonful much faster than usual.

"Can we have our surprise now please, Abuelita?" his eldest, Victoria, asked.

"Yes, come outside and see!"

James helped his ailing mother-in-law to her feet and held onto her arm as they followed the girls into the front yard. Even before he saw it, he heard the girls' exclamations of joy rise up into the air like bright bunches of balloons.

"Wow!"

"Is that for us?"

"It's the biggest bus I've seen in my whole life!"

Sure enough, a giant gleaming camper stood proudly by the curb. His father-in-law stood before it jangling the keys in his direction. "Your last chance to make a special memory before the new baby comes," he explained. "Go, make it a good one."

He winked and tossed the keys toward James, who caught them with ease.

"It's too much, Mama!" Gloria argued, but James could tell from the look on her face that she was quite pleased by the gesture.

"Hush now," her mother chided. "Go, enjoy yourselves. Just the six of you. Soon you will be seven, and the girls need this time besides. Your papa and brothers will take care of everything while you're away. When you come home, the nursery will have a fresh coat of paint and the house too."

Her father nodded. "Go. Take the weekend. We will be all right on our own for a few days."

Gloria cuddled with her daughters on the blanket they'd spread out in the grass, while James worked on getting a fire started.

"I'm hungry, Mama," Jacqueline said.

The baby kicked at the sound of its sister's voice, and Gloria smiled to herself. Even though this was supposed to be their last big hurrah before the baby joined them, she was still very much a part of this time as well. Gloria thought of the baby as a she, because, well, she and James had a track record and all.

"We'll eat soon. First Daddy has to get the fire going, then we'll roast hotdogs and marshmallows and corn. Doesn't that sound yummy?"

The baby kicked again, harder than before. "Hush, little one. You'll get some too." She giggled and tried to relax, despite the growing pain in her abdomen. Her daughters ran through the campgrounds and in and out of the RV, playing tag and getting out their pent up energy from the long drive.

The girls screeched with delight. Normally, the

sound of their fun would bring a smile to her face, but this time it shot straight through her brain causing a wicked headache. Then came a hard bump, knocking the wind right out of her. She looked to reprimand the daughter who had obviously run straight into her during play, but the three bigger girls were tearing through the camper, and Constance sat nearby playing with her favorite stuffed bear.

Kick.

The baby. Oh no, she...

Twist.

But Gloria wasn't due for another three weeks, and she always carried to term—a few days past it actually.

Sploosh.

Her water broke, leaving her with no other possibility. But they were at least an hour and a half from the nearest hospital, from Mama and home. And James...

A searing pain ripped through Gloria, and she cried out from both the pain and shock of it all.

Her daughters came bounding out of the trailer.

"Mama...?" She could hear tears in Jacqueline's voice as the little girl—the one who had always been the most nurturing of the bunch—pressed the back of her hand to her mother's forehead to check for fever.

"Mama, what's wrong?"

"The... baby..." Gloria huffed, having a hard time getting the words out.

That was when her hero arrived.

The moment James saw her, he dropped the bundle of sticks he'd been carrying to feed the fire and ran to her side.

"Girls," he said calmly. "Go inside. Victoria, get some water. Jacqueline, bring out the sleeping bags and towels. Beverly, mind Constance. The new baby has decided we shouldn't have all this fun without including him."

Gloria stopped worrying then and put all her trust in James and in God. Neither would let her or this baby down. She was sure of it.

"Victoria, can I trust you with a very big favor?" James asked when the girls returned with the supplies as requested. "I need you to help your sisters have their dinner and then put them to bed. Can you do that for me, sweetie?"

"Yes, Daddy." Her eyes darted toward her mother

and a frown crept across her small face. "Is—is Mama going to be okay?"

He laughed to help put her and the others at ease. "Of course, of course. The baby is on the way. I'll come in and wake you up once he's here, okay?"

"Okay." Her mind seemingly put at ease, Victoria skipped away, ushering each of her younger sisters into the van.

He poured some water into a cup for Gloria, then, when he was sure his daughters were out of earshot, asked, "Is everything okay, *mi corazon*? Should we move inside?"

She squeezed his hand and attempted to smile. "No, no, I want to be here under the stars. It's a nice change from all those times at home staring up at the ceiling."

"Should we drive back to town? I can—?"

She placed a hand on his arm as if to stop him from fussing. "I don't think we'll have enough time. This baby is not quite as patient as the rest."

"Patience is overrated." He settled down with her and began to massage her calves between the contractions. If he kept talking, perhaps she'd be distracted from the pain. He had nothing else to give her as an analgesic, so his words would have to be enough.

"I had to wait years—*years*—to meet you. The hardest thing I've ever done in my life. Maybe this baby feels the same. Nine months is too long to wait when it comes to meeting the most wonderful woman in the whole entire world."

He hadn't meant to get so sentimental on her, but as he watched her push through the pain of labor to bring them this beautiful gift of another perfect child, he just couldn't help it. As much as he was continually overwhelmed by his love for her, James felt his affection surge to even higher levels.

"You're the best thing that's ever happened to me," he said with tears in his eyes as he held tightly to his wife's hand. "Everything they put me through in that camp, all of it, was worth it, because it led me to you."

"James, stop." She attempted to let go of his hand.

He'd gotten too corny for her, but he wanted to make sure she knew. "I mean it, I love you so—"

"No, James. Stop. I love you too, but I need you to get ready. The baby's coming right now," she huffed. "We need to... focus... on... Aaaah!"

And their fifth child came screaming into the world, bright red, full of spirit, and...

"It's a boy," he whispered. Then louder, "Gloria,

it's a boy! Meet our son!" James cut the cord, then placed the baby on his mother's chest and covered them both with a blanket to protect them from the chilly night air.

"I'll be right back. I have to go tell the girls! Oh, they'll be so happy, Gloria. I'm so happy!" He kissed her forehead, then the baby's, leaving mother and son alone briefly so he could go get the rest of the family to share in this moment.

Gloria couldn't believe it. The baby was here, and a boy. Ever since she'd lost her brother, she'd known she wanted a son to raise in his honor. She also wanted James to have a boy of his own so he could experience all those important father-son bonding moments she knew he craved. Yes, he loved his girls with his entire heart, but a boy was special in a different way. And now they had one to call their own.

"Jacob Ricardo Morgan, that's what we'll call you," she told the baby, pressing him to her bosom. "Named after two great men. You've got a lot to live up to, little one, but don't worry, Mama will be there to support you every step of the way."

The baby latched on just as her other children emerged from the camper and tore over to where she and the baby lay nuzzled together.

"Oh, wow! We have a brother!" they exclaimed.

"Mama, can I sing the baby a song?" Jacqueline asked, pressing her face close to Gloria's.

"I think he'd like that," she answered, smiling up at her girls.

"I want to sing too," Beverly cried.

"We should all sing. After all, he's *all* of our brother."

James laughed and mussed up Victoria's hair. "That's a good point, Vicky, and what should we sing to him?"

She thought for a few moments, then her eyes lit up and she spoke so fast he could hardly understand her. "Since we're camping, I think we should sing Kumbaya. I think the baby will like it. It's kind of like a lullaby. Right, Daddy?"

"Oh, yes, yes!" Beverly shouted, joining in Victoria's excitement.

But Jacqueline pouted, "I don't know that song..."

"Come here," Gloria said reaching out her free arm. "It's an easy song to learn. We'll all teach you."

The girls cuddled with their mother as James

finally brought the fire to life. The sound of their voices mixing together as the heat crackled before them was the most beautiful thing James had heard in his entire life.

"James, come hold your son," Gloria urged once they had all sung a few rounds and the baby had finished his first meal outside the womb. And when she placed the tiny bundle—the smallest yet of all his children—in James's arm, he knew he was a goner.

The baby stretched his arms forward and accidentally scratched himself near the eye.

"Hey, hey, buddy. Careful," he warned. "You'll need those eyes. There's so much beauty in this world, so much you still need to see."

He wrapped his son in a blanket, then returned to his wife's side. "Should we get you to a hospital?" he asked.

"I feel fine, James. No need to go just yet. Besides..." She lay her head on his shoulder and looked up at the stars. "I don't want this moment to end just yet."

He chuckled softly. "Mama was right, just as always. This will make the perfect memory."

WHEN I FALL IN LOVE, PART II

The bright Texas sun shone through the drawn curtains in Deborah's room, forcing her to awaken before she was ready. During all her years in Alaska, she'd grown accustomed to normally being able to sleep in if she wanted to—not the case in Texas, where the sun rose early and didn't go to bed without a fight.

She'd only visited Abilene once before deciding to make it her home. Of course, she missed her children and grandchildren desperately, but she also needed a fresh start. Needed to escape the grief that hung over Anchorage like an eternal veil.

First she'd lost her son and daughter-in-law

there and then her husband, tarnishing even the happier memories that were tied to the place she'd once called home.

Abilene, she liked. It reminded her of her hometown growing up, of the 1950s, of simpler, happier times before life got so confusing.

Deborah's knees ached as she lifted herself from bed and shrugged into her housecoat. She prepared a fresh glass of iced tea with a sprig of mint then padded out onto her wrap-around porch to say good morning to the neighbors.

She'd never have guessed she'd enjoy living in a retirement village, but life had always found new ways to take her by surprise.

Age and time changed everything, it seemed. Oh, Rip would laugh if he could see her now. Garnishing her tea with mint and wearing an embroidered housecoat—of all the crazy things.

But Rip had nodded off one night and never woken again. He'd had a smile plastered across his face when she found him, and that had filled her with both despair and joy. Rip was finally free of the pain he'd been trying to hide since the war, but he'd also left her alone to face life on her own.

And thus she lost the second great love of her life.

At nearly eighty years old, she doubted she'd find another, which meant she didn't have much left to do other than enjoy every minute of her life and wait for it to finally be over. At least with Rip, though, she'd had closure. They'd lived more than fifty years together in marital bliss—well, normally it was bliss. They'd journeyed through life together and said goodbye when his had ended.

Not like with James.

She shuddered as she remembered receiving the news that James had gone missing in action over Korea. Even all these years later she still couldn't forget it. Sometimes she felt guilty that not all of her fondest memories were tied to Rip, but then again she'd given him everything.

James never had the chance to receive the full effect of her love.

A tiny moving van—well, tiny as far as these things went—turned onto the street and came to a stop a few houses down.

Oh, goodie, the new neighbors had finally arrived.

Anyone would be better than old lady Bernstein —of that Deborah was certain.

She watched with interest as a handsome young man hopped out of the truck and began hauling boxes to the porch. Although he was young enough to be her grandson, he was pleasant to look at and she refused to deny herself the pleasure of watching his muscles bulge beneath the weight of the packages.

Something about him excited her, and it wasn't just his good looks. The way he moved swiftly and surely, the way his smile seemed both self-assured and clumsy. He reminded her of...

"Slow down, slow down. You'll tucker yourself right out," an older man called from within the van. Deborah watched as the door pushed open and a pair of trousered legs emerged—followed by the man to whom they belonged.

At once, it was as if she were seventeen years old again, sipping on a strawberry shake at the local soda fountain.

James stood right in front of her, sending a smile her way.

James's feet were glued to the sidewalk, or maybe the Earth's gravitational pull had suddenly strengthened making them too heavy to lift. Whatever the reason, he was stuck in place, unable to tear his eyes away from the beauty who sat before him wearing a housecoat and sipping on an iced tea.

Deborah. Deborah, it was really her.

He smiled, and she smiled back. Neither spoke.

He'd tried to find her after the war, if only to tell her that he was all right. She'd left town though, and he'd found Gloria, and... none of that mattered just then.

Because here she was, every bit as beautiful as the day he'd first laid eyes on her at the soda shop. Crow's feet tugged at the corners of her eyes, indicating she'd lived a life filled with happiness—just as he'd always hoped she would. Her white hair shone in the morning sun, casting a soft glow about her.

Since he couldn't move, he needed to say something. Otherwise, an eternity would pass as they stood—and sat—staring at each other.

"Deborah?"

"Hello, James." She smiled, rising slowly from her chair. She walked over to him, never once taking her eyes from his. When she stood but a few paces away, she asked, "Is it really you, or have I finally lost my mind?"

He laughed, just as he had all those years ago, carefree and light in her presence. "It's really me."

"So you didn't die in the war like everybody said?"

He shook his head. "I tried to find you, to tell you I'd made it out alive, but you were already gone."

"I'm here now."

"Yes, you are." And before he could lose the nerve, he asked her once again, "Deborah, may I kiss you?"

"Yes, but it's not goodbye this time either. You got that?"

"I don't ever want to say goodbye again," he whispered into her cheek as they closed their arms around each other in a long overdue embrace.

"Then don't."

He brushed his lips against hers, unlocking both their pasts and their futures in one perfect gesture.

YOU MAKE ME FEEL SO YOUNG

Deborah's hands shook as she lifted the tiny pearl earrings up to her earlobes. She'd worn this same pair all those years ago when she and James first met at the local soda fountain, when she was nothing more than a girl. Would he remember?

She grimaced as she eyed herself in the mirror. While she understood she was attractive for a woman of her age, she still could hardly believe that the wrinkled face staring back through the glass was actually her own. Where had the soft blush of her cheeks gone? Why did her eyes look so small and squinty next to the ubiquitous crows' feet that tugged at the corners? Her lips, while constantly glossed, were never quite smooth, and her pretty blond hair had settled into a dull whitish color.

But despite the arthritis, the wrinkles, and other omnipresent reminders of old age, Deborah still felt young, girlish, alive as she readied herself for her evening out with James. It had been so long since she'd last prepared for a romantic evening out. In fact, it had been years since Rip was still well enough to accompany her out for...

Rip.

She'd sworn she would never—could never—love another man, not when she'd spent her entire life with one whom she'd loved so dearly and who in turn had given her everything she'd ever wanted from life: love, family, even adventure. Of course, she could rationalize the way all the other widows in her community did.

It's what he would have wanted, but was it? She cringed whenever she dared to think about how Rip would be doing, were their situations reversed. He'd never have moved on, not in a million years. Let alone two.

But then again, James wasn't a *new* love. He'd taken her heart years before she'd met and fallen for Rip.

She lifted her eyes toward the lace-adorned

window and peered outside. James and his grandson were still moving boxes back and forth from the truck to the house. The poor dears must have been exhausted, and yet... James still insisted on taking her out that very night—as if he couldn't wait another moment to continue their story.

It was just being neighborly, really. She'd show him the sights of their humble retirement village, which wouldn't take too long at all. And when they were through, she'd thank him for keeping her such good company for the evening—as she had no doubt he would—and then she'd bid him good night.

There. It was decided. No more feeling guilty. No more wondering *what if?*

Buh buh. Buh-buh. Buhbuh. Buhbuhbuhbuhbuhbuh.

James heart beat faster and faster while he stood on Deborah's front porch and waited for her to open the door. How long had he waited for this very moment? It felt like years, but also as if no time had passed at all. He still remembered everything about her, or at least the seventeen-year-old version of her: how she wrote poetry, loved strawberry malts, was carefree, exuberant. And he could see all those things within Deborah still, though they seemed buried beneath a cautious exterior.

Life did that sometimes, took more than it gave. How he hoped he'd read the situation wrong. Because for him, life had given in spades, just as it was doing again, offering up his first love in a tidy suburban package mere months after he'd lost his wife so suddenly to the stroke.

The door creaked open, revealing Deborah in a soft, floral sundress and fuzzy cream cardigan. She wore pearls both around her neck and upon her ears, an image that took him straight back to that night.

She noticed him staring and reached a hand up to her ear. "The very same," she said with a smile. "Are those for me?"

James looked down at the edible bouquet held firmly between his palms, which were growing sweatier by the second. It was as if he were a boy again! "I-I figured these would be nicer than simple flowers. Is strawberry still your favorite?"

"Oh, how very sweet." Deborah reached out and took the arrangement of carved strawberries resembling a bouquet of tulips. Her fingers brushed his. A spark, one he knew she felt as he did.

A flush rose to her cheeks, and she excused herself to put James' gift in the fridge.

It really was as if no time had passed at all, as if they were children again. Was this God's way of thanking him for answering his country's call to serve and protect? By giving him yet another chance to know great love?

He checked his breath by huffing into his palm, then popped a sugar-free Tic Tac anyway. Only the best for his girl. Oh, how he hoped she would have him.

Deborah reappeared and slid the door shut behind her. "All right," she said. "I'm ready."

James put one hand in the lapel of his jacket and crooked the other arm, inviting Deborah to take hold. A moment's hesitation crossed between them, but then she smiled and accepted his arm.

And they were together. Finally together again.

He'd remembered too, that much was clear as they wove through their neighborhood toward the tiny downtown area where speakers, musicians, and other types of entertainers often came to put on a show for their community of active seniors.

James reached for her hand as if it were the most natural thing in the entire world, as if they'd been taking these walks together the whole of their lives. "I want to know everything I missed," he said. "Tell me, how has your life been?"

Deborah hesitated. She loved the life she'd lived with Rip, but that didn't mean there was nothing she'd change, if only given the chance.

"Did you have kids?" He smiled and gave her hand a reassuring squeeze.

"Five. All boys."

"I had five too. Four girls and a boy. They all think I moved too far away from home, coming here, but it's only really an hour's drive. Does your family live close by?"

Deborah shook her head. "Wayne, Arthur, Fred, and Kurtis live back in Anchorage. Lewis... in Heaven."

He stopped walking and wrapped her into an effortless hug. "I'm so sorry. I didn't know."

And even though she'd lost Lewis and his wife Shirley so many years ago, the pain still hung just beneath the surface. If there were some secret way to recover from the loss of a child, she had yet to discover it.

"I'm fine. Really." She pulled out of his hug and forced a smile to her face.

"Hey," James said, pointing down the block. "Gonzo's. Is that place any good?"

Now her smile came easily. "Only the best."

He reached for her hand again and pulled her excitedly toward the tiny Coney Island diner. "Do you still like malted milks?" A twinkle lit up his eyes.

"Oh, yes, I do." And she giggled, the earlier gravity of their conversation already swept clean away.

They took a seat by the window, and James called the waitress over. "One strawberry malt, and..."—turning to Deborah—"I hope you don't mind, but I'll have to join you with a Diet Coke." He cupped a hand to the side of his face and whispered, "Diabetes."

"You know..." he continued once the waitress had left to prepare their order. "It's funny we should meet now after all this time, don't you think? I've found that where we are now is a lot like where we were back then, transitioning between two phases in life. It's that same freedom, being able to make a new life for ourselves, having so many options before us."

Deborah nodded, but she wasn't sure she agreed.

Back then, she'd had no pain to anchor her, no regrets to hide.

"And, in case you were wondering, the feelings are all still there, same as before, as if they never left, only got tucked away for a while. I'm still crazy about you, Deborah Walker."

She felt heat rise to her cheeks. It was so natural with James, and—yes—she had to agree that the feelings were every bit as intense today as they'd been fifty years ago. Perhaps more so since James was now cutting in on the lonely dance her life had become.

"It's Deborah Rockwell now," she corrected, reaching her hands across the table to hold each of his. "And I'm crazy about you, too."

❦

Ahh, there she was at last. Before he had only suspected, but now James knew for sure; that carefree girl still lived inside her, even though she'd clearly experienced more pain than any one person ever deserved to suffer—especially one so sweet, so wonderful.

Another effervescent memory bubbled to the surface. "Do you still write poetry?" he asked while the waitress set their drinks down on the table before them.

She coughed then laughed at herself. "I do, actually. Poetry and some longer pieces as well. I'm working on my memoirs now."

"So you really did it? You got to do what you love for a living?"

She nodded. "Yes, I got to raise my children, and then my grandchildren too. Writing has always been with me, but it's also always been second to family. Until now, that is. I have so much time on my hands, it seems silly not to spend it productively." She waved a hand in front of her face as if to dismiss the topic. "Anyway, tell me what it is you've done all these years. I always wondered... When you didn't come back from the war... I'm so glad you're okay."

Squeeze. Her fingers were warm as she clapped both hands around his once more and smiled.

"I tried to find you, to tell you I was okay. But by the time I made it back round to town, they'd said you'd moved to Alaska. I tried to write, but my letters always ended up returned to sender."

"It doesn't matter. What matters is that you're here now, that you're okay."

"I'm more than okay, Deborah." He held her eyes

with his, earnestness in his gaze. Could she see how much she'd done for him simply by being here now?

A few wordless moments passed between them before Deborah pushed herself out from the booth and reached for James' hand once more. "Come with me. I have something beautiful to show you."

And they were off again, weaving past the shops and condos, making their way deeper into the village.

"This is my favorite spot in the entire neighborhood," she said, directing him to a majestic white fountain tucked away in the middle of the community, far away from the main hustle and bustle. "I come here to think. Sometimes to write. To wish." She turned her face away from his and looked up at the sun. "I've often wished that you..." She stopped, smiled.

"I know." And he did know, because he'd often thought of her as well, hoping that life had turned out well for her, wondering if their paths might ever cross again. And now here they were.

He reached a shaking hand into his pocket and groped about until he found two spare coins, bright copper pennies, shiny as the day they were made. He handed one to Deborah. "Will you make a wish with me now?"

She nodded, as if she'd known the request was coming. "Of course."

They stood silent before the fountain side by side as they each held their lucky charms securely within a fist, then entrusted them to the water. He knew better than to ask what she had wished for, so instead he bent forward and began to remove his loafers.

"What are you doing?"

The grin hadn't left her face since that special moment at Gonzo's.

"I'm going wading. And so are you. C'mon."

He helped her off with her shoes and stockings and then escorted her into the shallow pool of water.

"You are positively...well, you're something else all right." She giggled and splashed some water his way.

He splashed back, joining in her laughter. And before they knew it a full-on water fight had ensued. James hadn't laughed so hard in a long time, but it was easy with Deborah—everything was easy with Deborah.

"Okay, okay, truce." He lifted his hands in surrender, and his wet shirt clung to his chest.

"You're just saying that because I'm winning."

She chuckled as she sent another plume of water his way.

But he didn't let that stop him. He closed the distance between them. "You win," he said, wrapping his arms around her. "But so do I."

She leaned forward and placed a sweet kiss on his lips, pulled away, then returned, deepening the kiss.

If he closed his eyes, James could swear he'd returned to that very night fifty years ago under the stars.

The night air began to grow chilly, more so because of their wet clothes and skin.

"Care to join me for some evening tea?" Deborah asked as they were stuffing their feet back into their shoes and socks. "Mind you, it's iced tea. But I do have a batch without sugar."

Back at her condo, she poured James a tall glass of tea and added a lemon wedge and mint for garnish. "Still a mite chilly, isn't it?" She turned to fetch her favorite quilt from the armchair in the other room.

"Did you make that?" James asked, his eyes wide

with admiration as she sat down close to him and draped the blanket across their laps.

"I did. With my granddaughters Charlie and Mandy. It was our special project a few summers back." She didn't mention how she had raised her granddaughters clear up from childhood after their parents had died. That would come later. She had no doubt about that. But now was a time for sharing feelings, dreams—just as it had been on their first date so many years back. They could catch up on the fine details another time.

"So you write, you quilt, you splash around in fountains... What don't you do?" James laughed softly and rubbed her knee to help warm it up.

"It's true, I've done quite a lot in my day. But there's still so much more I'd like to cross off the ol' bucket list before I go." Funny how easy it was to reference her own death these days and to do so without feeling the slightest bit awkward or sad. Death was just a fact, an eventuality. Neither good nor bad—not anymore.

"Oh, a bucket list, eh? What do you have left to do?"

"Well, I'd like to see Paris. Somehow I never made it over there. And I really must learn to make a spinach quiche I can be proud of. Oh, and I definitely want to learn how to bind my own books. That way when I'm finished with my memoir, I can make myself a copy." She stopped and looked over toward James. "But that's just me. I always have something else I'm meaning to get to. How about you? What's on your list?"

He twisted his mouth into a fine line as he thought. "It's funny. I've never actually stopped to think about it. But now that you ask, it's easy to think of things I'd like to do if there's time. Like ride a horse again. Climb to the top of the Rockies, if my body will let me. Maybe take an RV cross-country and see the sights."

"See the big sights or the little ones?"

"What do you mean?"

"Like would you choose to visit the Grand Canyon or the world's largest ball of twine?"

James laughed from his belly. "Now that you mention it, I've seen the Grand Canyon, but I've never seen that ball of twine. I pick the latter."

"Me too." Deborah rested her head on James' chest and tucked her feet up under her on the sofa. Even with their frail, inflexible bodies, they still fit together quite rightly. Perhaps it would be okay if she allowed herself to fall in love with James again, because, after all, she'd never really stopped loving him in the first place. Rip could rest easy knowing she had someone to share her adventures with, someone to keep her company as she waded through this life and prepared to meet up with him again in the next.

James bent down and placed a kiss on the top of her head. "This has been the best day," he whispered.

She smiled, delighting in the spicy, woodsy scent of him. "The best part is knowing we don't have to say goodbye ever again, not if we don't want to."

"I don't want to."

Deborah didn't want to either. She'd been lonely long enough. "Stay with me?" she whispered.

James wrapped his arms tighter around her. "Always."

SIGN UP FOR EVEN MORE FREE STORIES AND UPLIFTING MESSAGES FROM MELISSA AT WWW. MELSTORM.COM/GIFT

Sign up for free stories, fun updates, and uplifting messages from Melissa at www.MelStorm.com/gift

* * *

The Church Dogs of Charleston

A very special litter of Chihuahua puppies born on Christmas day is adopted by the local church and immediately set to work as tiny therapy dogs.

Little Loves

Mini Miracles

Dainty Darlings

* * *

The Sled Dog Series

Get ready to fall in love with a special pack of working and retired sled dogs, each of whom change their new owners' lives for the better.

Let There Be Love

Let There Be Light

Let There Be Life

Season of Mercy

* * *

The First Street Church Romances

Sweet and wholesome small town love stories with the community church at their center make for the perfect feel-good reads!

Love's Prayer

Love's Promise

Love's Prophet

Love's Vow

Love's Trial

* * *

The Memory Ranch Romances

This new Sled Dogs-spinoff series harnesses the restorative power of both horses and love at Elizabeth Jane's therapeutic memory ranch.

Memories of Home

Memories of Heaven

Memories of Healing

* * *

Sweet Promise Press

What's our Sweet Promise? It's to deliver the heartwarming, entertaining, clean, and wholesome reads you love with every single book.

Saving Sarah

Flirting with the Fashionista

* * *

Stand-Alone Novels and Novellas

Whether climbing ladders in the corporate world or taking care of things at home, every woman has a story to tell.

A Mother's Love

A Colorful Life

Love & War

* * *

Special Collections & Boxed Sets

From light-hearted comedies to stories about finding hope in the darkest of times, these special boxed editions offer a great way to catch up or to fall in love with Melissa Storm's books for the first time.

The Sled Dog Series: Books 1-3

The First Street Church Romances: Books 1-3

The Church Dogs of Charleston: Books 1-3

Finding Mr. Happily Ever After: Books 1-5

The Alaska Sunrise Romances: A 9-Book Sweet Romance Collection

Melissa Storm is a mother first, and everything else second. Writing is her way of showing her daughter just how beautiful life can be, when you pay attention to the everyday wonders that surround us. So, of course, Melissa's USA Today bestselling fiction is highly personal and often based on true stories.

Melissa loves books so much, she married fellow author Falcon Storm. Between the two of them, there are always plenty of imaginative, awe-inspiring stories to share. Melissa and Falcon also run a number of book-related businesses together, including LitRing, Sweet Promise Press, Novel Publicity, Your Author Engine, and the Author Site. When she's not reading, writing, or child-rearing, Melissa spends time relaxing at home in the company of a seemingly unending quantity of dogs and a rescue cat named Schrödinger.

GET IN TOUCH!

www.MelStorm.com

author@melstorm.com

Made in the USA
Columbia, SC
28 March 2020

90095538R00134